I
AM
AGATHA

I
AM
AGATHA

NANCY FOLEY

First published in Great Britain in 2026 by
Serpent's Tail,
an imprint of Profile Books Ltd
29 Cloth Fair
London
EC1A 7JQ

www.serpentstail.com

First published in in the United States of America in 2026 by
Avid Reader Press, an imprint of Simon & Schuster, LLC

Interior design by Ritika Karnik

1 3 5 7 9 10 8 6 4 2

Printed and bound in Great Britain by
CPI Group (UK) Ltd, Croydon CR0 4YY

The moral right of the author has been asserted.

A CIP catalogue record for this book is available from the British Library.

Our product safety representative in the EU is BGC Sustainability & Compliance,
7 avenue du Général Leclerc, Paris, 75014, France https://baldwinglobalconsulting.com

ISBN 978 1 80522 881 3
eISBN 978 1 80522 882 0

MIX
Paper | Supporting
responsible forestry
FSC® C013604

for Kevin

ONE

1

I WAS DRIVING IN MY PICKUP with the windows rolled down for the breeze. In the distance Mesa Portales shifted and rippled in the heat. People say New Mexico is layered in reds and browns and sage greens, but they are mistaken. It's limned by ghostly pinks and blues, and the light is of a register sharper than other places. The sun leaves little hidden, and everything is bleached and broken down, exposed. I can see things coming from a long way off.

But I didn't see Alice coming. On the road ahead was her house, crumbling around the edges yet buffeted by great swooning whirls of flowers. In the backyard was a path leading to a wooden cross atop a mounded grave. Beyond that were acres of sagebrush and piñon, rattlesnakes resting in puddles of shade.

I didn't love Alice then and so I didn't think of her. But there she was at the side of the road, trotting more than walking, chasing after three chickens that squawked and scattered just out of reach when she tried to shoo them with her hand or otherwise make a grab for them.

I eased the pickup over and turned off the engine. At the time I wondered how someone who had lived out here her entire life, more than six decades, couldn't manage her own chickens. Now I think

Alice's brain was just beginning to let go of trivial things, so that the more important things could stay. A prioritizing. Last spring, to solve the chicken problem, she wrung all their necks and we ate them roasted, barbecued, boiled.

I got out of my pickup. I am older than Alice, yet easily scooped up the chickens and threw them over the fence, one, two, three. I have quite a bit of experience in this department from Saskatchewan. The chickens landed clucking and complaining before hobbling off to peck in the weeds.

Thank you, Alice said. And who are you?

I laughed when she said this. It was true we'd met only briefly when I'd signed the lease two years earlier. But I stick out around here. Now and then a graduate student like Veronica finds her way to me, and one day a magazine writer appeared, so dehydrated that I thought he might die on me. I pointed him to a jug of water and a few blackberries in an old margarine container, and once revived he made a poor joke about how far off the grid he'd come just to learn more about it. But I don't care for jokes on a serious topic—if you look properly at my work you will see that there is no grid at all, there is only a feeling that comes over you—and so I sent him away directly.

The point I'm making is that people find me simply by asking around in town. I am noticed and commented upon, which is nothing new. But Alice had not been noticing or commenting on me. In fact she didn't think of or remember me at all. Yet once I was in front of her, she trusted me immediately with her important things.

Would you like to see Lorna? she said.

I could tell right away that this wasn't a casual question, that casual questions were not of interest to her, and I approved of this. But who was Lorna to me? Nobody. At that time I had no sense of whether Lorna was a girl or a goat or something else entirely. And so I hesitated. I wanted to get back in my pickup and do what needed doing in town and after that go back home to Mesa Portales. Summers up there I can watch lightning storms stretch their electric fingers for miles in all directions.

But Alice smiled, she patted her thigh as if encouraging a shy dog, she held out her hand and said, Come. She had the air of a patient schoolteacher about her, which in fact she once had been. I tried not to hold her hand but she insisted, and as we stepped onto her property the chickens smoothed their ruffled feathers back into their wings.

IT WAS THE NAVAJO BOY who gave Lorna the silver and turquoise thunderbird brooch that Alice wears on her shirt collar, and it was the first thing Alice attended to when she invited me into her home, as if it were part of dressing up for company. She crossed the room to the clock on the fireplace mantel, turned the tiny knob on its case door, and took out the brooch. She struggled with the clasp and so I helped her. My fingers trembled when she leaned in close, and I felt a tender thing reaching out to me. I looked up to find her gaze on my mouth, but then she closed her eyes, as if I had caught her in something.

This Navajo boy had loved Lorna and she had loved him. Alice herself had a fondness for the boy because he was kind and decent and handsome. But even so it was impossible, because who could change the world? Not Lorna, so delicate, so agreeable.

Our daughter is not going to live in a hogan, Alice's husband had said. She is not going to fry bread over a woodstove or ride in a horse cart to the grocery store. He threw Lorna's things in a suitcase and enrolled her in a court stenography course in Albuquerque. Everything about this was a smart move, he said, because Lorna's future husband would thereby be a rich lawyer, as her employment would put her in their way on a daily basis.

But Lorna didn't catch a rich lawyer. Instead a man indicted for armed robbery spotted her during his trial. This man got off on a technicality and came back to the courthouse to sweep Lorna off her feet, because he swore he couldn't bear to be another moment of the day without her. Alice called it love, but to me it sounded like suffocation. Also this man had tried to rob a corner store, which made me wonder at Lorna's choices. Why not a jewel heist or museum theft? Both much more ambitious dreams.

The brooch's turquoise stone was small and oval, true like sky, mounted on the thunderbird's tarnished belly. Alice touched it gently with her fingertip. Then she led me down the garden path to Lorna.

Alice's yard was humble, cluttered with potted plants and scraps of wood and metal for things already broken or not yet built. The path was bordered by clipped grass, a tidy strangeness. Many times since I've watched her trim that grass with a pair of scissors, and over the years she has made an increasingly uneven hash of it.

She walked without looking back at me because she was confident that I would follow. Not many of us still have our graceful walk, if we ever had it at all. But Alice did. Her back was straight and her strides were long. She said, My husband passed. Things slid across her face: first a flash of triumph and next a mask of sorrow. Also she gestured vaguely over her heart, presumably identifying the space where her dead husband could have been expected to have one. I was not surprised at this suggestion of heart failure as his was rotten, I am sure. Certainly he helped me get the lease for Mesa Portales, but many times since I have thought, May the Devil take him. Each time I have this thought, it is immediately followed by the greatest satisfaction, because of course the Devil already has.

Alice took my arm and guided me to a pair of rickety chairs alongside a grave covered in lush grass and dotted with violets. A stand of lilac bushes, long since bloomed, shaded the grave; the land beyond the backyard was brown and dry in those months of late summer, yet the lilac leaves were strangely firm and dewy green, and I felt as if in an unnatural place. Also I was too large for the chair but was momentarily inhabited with politeness and sat down just to please her. I suppose to her this closeness felt companionable, but for me it wasn't, not yet.

Lorna's name was carved in flowers and curlicues on a wooden cross, the letters almost impossible to read in their fuss and ornamentation. *June 5, 1937–August 29, 1958.* Thirteen years ago this month, Alice said, and rested her hand on the cross.

I imagined a Sleeping Beauty in the earth and felt an uneasy chill. What is wrong with fire, with ashes and dust?

Lorna was kind and sweet, Alice said. She was the sun, the moon, and the stars.

The words Alice spoke were cliché and sentimental, I'm sorry to say that. They made me unable to know Lorna at all. I winced when she said those things, and she mistook this gesture for sorrow at

Lorna's passing. Well, I did feel sorrow for Alice, but also I know about ghost children. There was one in my own family. It was named Ellis and lived only two days. As the firstborn it made a large impression on my mother, and we subsequent children suffered in its shadow. It remained forever a mystery to us whether Ellis was a boy or a girl. We children did not know and for reasons mysterious to ourselves were afraid to ask, and no one ever told us; at times this topic would consume all our thoughts. The fact is I don't believe in lingering excessively over dead people, because it is an affront to the living ones still among us.

I KISSED ALICE FOR THE first time later that afternoon as she wrestled with the wringer washer in the laundry nook off the kitchen. It was easy to feel free in this laundry nook, with its straightforward purpose, no frills or knickknacks, only the gleam and thump of the metal tub with its soapy churn. I admired the gentle pulse at Alice's throat and her dark hair threaded with white, and it came over me that I should kiss her. But when I put my hand on her waist, she startled and exclaimed, I thought you were my husband's ghost and it gave me quite a start!

That was not worth hearing—I did not like it whatsoever—and so I kissed her to make us both forget it. At first her lips were firm, but warmed and softened as she kissed me back. Also she laughed, laughter that was deep and throaty and with a liveliness in it. This laugh was her true self.

Before I left, Alice invited me to meet her for a swim the next day, at the old reservoir that had been a favorite place of hers since she was a child. Most years growing up, she told me, she had two dresses and wore each one three days in a row. In summer evenings she walked to the reservoir to scrub out whichever dress needed washing. Other girls had only one dress, and they crouched at the reservoir's edge in their underthings, washed their lone dress, and wore it home wet. Alice thought this practical, but her mother forbade her to wash both her dresses at the same time, for fear that anyone seeing her in a wet dress might think she was the possessor of only one.

Alice said that she would walk to the reservoir because a walk was one of the dearest things in life to her. Never a day passed where she did not embark on one or two. Would you like to walk there with me? she asked.

But I shook my head. I'd run away from home at the age of thirteen, drifted through many parts of this country and walked more miles than I ever care to again. I had no wish to revisit what was a necessity of my youth and an activity that I associate with hardship. I'll meet you there, I said, and I won't be late. She blushed when I took her hand. I could feel this lovely blush in her fingers, which pinked and grew damp in my own.

I wanted no engine sputters or exhaust fumes or stirring up of dust to ruin whatever pleasing atmosphere might be possible upon my arrival to the reservoir. By this I mean I had hopes. So I drove in my pickup until in the near distance I saw the dark smudge of trees that marked out the water, and then I walked the rest of the way.

Everywhere was the jump and whir of grasshoppers. I carried a treat in a small burlap sack, and I thought of Alice as I walked. She'd said her childhood home had been nearby but burned down in a lightning strike years ago. Later she would take me there and show me a crumbling outline of blackened bricks. Here was the kitchen, here was the room where the seven of us slept, she said. Here was where we kept the rabbits for meat, I never tasted steak until I was grown. She held my hand in the dry yellow valley ringed with blue mountains, and we listened to its quiet.

The sagebrush hid the reservoir from view until I came upon it. I took off my boots and sat in the shade of a willow tree that trailed its branches into the water. I imagined Alice as a young girl: the cooling evening, her slender wrists dipping into the water to scrub her dress, her mother's impractical pride. Also I thought of myself at the same moment in time, when women gave me odd jobs in exchange for a meal and afterward watched from the porch to be sure I went on my way. I once snuck into a schoolhouse and searched through the lunch pails, my heart twisting at the sound of the children playing outside, their whooping cries moving through me like colorful birds.

Alice pushed through the sagebrush and stepped out of her shoes. She'd brought cornbread wrapped in a cloth and pushed a jar of milk into the mud to keep it cool. The swing of her dress was close enough to touch. But when I reached out my hand, she hesitated and turned away.

We stripped down, she to her underthings and me to my entirety. The reservoir folded up around us as we glided in, our movements making gentle waves that lapped back and forth between us. I felt these waves as a signal of some kind.

Alice dipped her head back briefly so that her hair was wet. Were you ever married? she asked.

Not me.

You never wanted to be?

I never wanted to be.

I did want to be, she said.

The night of her fifteenth birthday Alice quietly took her older sister's Sunday dress off its hook. She put the dress on in the dark and slipped outside, followed a deep arroyo that snaked a mile in the dark. As she walked she gathered the dress in her hands to keep off the dust. Her soon-to-be husband waited for her where the arroyo opened to the road. He held a bouquet of white daisies, their petals luminous under the moon. But the pickup broke down on the road to Santa Fe, and so there was no quiet motel, no soft bed. Instead he carried her from the front seat to the flatbed, and in the night her sister's dress was spoiled and Alice cried; the sky had gone black with no stars. Next morning a car stopped to offer help with the engine, and they made it to the magistrate by noon, before her mother had a say in any of it.

I thought he was a gentleman, she said, but I wasn't right about that. It's a sadness to me. I suppose it might have been nice at times, but I can't remember those parts anymore. Now that he has passed, I am trying to forget him. In my head I am trying to be free.

Then she nodded at me, as if wanting a story in return.

I told her how at sixteen I met Ma Binney and her widows on the road to Wichita. When Ma Binney saw me she held up a hand and all the widows quieted behind her. These widows were little sparrows and Ma Binney a hawk, her hair long and cloud white with the end of her braid coiled into the breast pocket of her jacket. But her face was young and at that time she was not yet twenty-five. No widow had fewer years than Ma Binney, but still she was the greatest in age among them, it was something in her very bones.

Ma Binney inspected me as the widows twittered behind her. You better come along with us, she finally said, as you sure look hungry, and we'll have supper in a while.

At night they sang and passed a hat in the pickers' camps. They kept to hymns. No love songs, Ma Binney said, because I'm not in the business of making folks cry. I held a handkerchief so she could wipe her forehead in the heat. She stood very straight while singing but between songs slouched slightly and ran her fingers idly up and down her braid. She looked over at me boldly, her eyes like flames.

When the singing was done Ma Binney brought me back to her tent and cut up a tomato, put it between two slices of bread, and served it to me on a china plate taken from a wooden chest next to her bedroll. Eat up, sweetheart, she said. Her words recalled to me a forgotten place, and I cleaned my plate without a word. Afterward she wiped the plate on her shirttail and put it back in the wooden chest. I asked, Did your hair turn white from losing your husband? She laughed long and loud at that. I was breathless to be so near to her.

She invited me to sleep on the bedroll with her, and in the dim of night her face was a craggy mountain beneath a snowy nightcap. She turned toward me, propped her head in one hand. Where do you come from? she asked. But I wouldn't say because I had grown more watchful in my time alone and didn't believe in giving things away.

What do we do now? I asked her instead.

She touched my cheek. She said that I should look only at her and never away, that a river existed inside me, full of power, and she would set it free. I was only briefly surprised when everything she said proved true, as I had already dreamed of its existence. Afterward she pulled a rough blanket over us and fell asleep, but not before boasting that I would never forget her. I lay in the dark with my heart now beating strongly, and my true life with it.

Some of the widows had feelings for Ma Binney, while others turned to me. When we were quiet together the widows told me about men they loved who left, about men who stayed when they weren't wanted, also about children who died or grew up ungrateful. I saw that they were happiest when they could weep, so I did not comfort them. I sketched their portraits in exchange for butterscotch candy, pieces of soap, or darned socks, and once a frayed silk camisole that I traded away for a man's undershirt. The widows swapped these portraits like valentines, and never since have I enjoyed such satisfaction in the market for my work.

In Nebraska Ma Binney presented me with a banged-up tin case of watercolor paints, the colors cracked like dried-up rouge. Go on now, paint me something, she said, and by something she meant herself. There isn't a person alive who doesn't know their good side, and Ma Binney offered me her left one straight off. But I closed the tin and turned away because I knew by the feeling inside me that painting her wasn't in me to do. I drew when it humored me, when I had a pencil and a bit of paper, and at the time it was never more than that.

At a revival tent near Lincoln, I saw a dark-haired girl in a blue dress who rang the bell for the start of the meeting. I discovered that two people can look at each other and right away understand they want something. We met at night in a grassy hollow at the edge of a pasture, and her skin lit up like prairie fire when I touched her. Afterward we lay on our backs and I pointed out the fingernail moon. She said, That woman whose thumb you're under looks rough.

I'm under no one's thumb, I said, surprised.

The girl was disbelieving. Why it's clear as day you are.

As she spoke those words I knew that she was right, and I did not like it.

Where you been? Ma Binney asked crossly when I slipped back into her bed, but I wouldn't answer, because all my thoughts had turned against her.

The next day the revival tent was gone, along with the dark-haired girl. By suppertime I had decided I was done with Ma Binney and her widows. When I said good-bye, Ma Binney hauled off and slapped me. The widows held her back and also gave me boiled sweets to take along. I didn't ration them as advised but sucked on one after another until it was all behind me.

Alice was thoughtful, then asked the only question that truly mattered to her. But did you ever love her, this Ma Binney?

No.

Who have you loved then, as a sweetheart?

I searched back in my life but could only shake my head.

Alice was silent for a moment, then said in a voice full of doubt, Your Ma Binney sounds like quite a character.

The banality of her words about Ma Binney was terrible. I dove under the water and held my breath as long as I could. Looking up, I saw the slow suspended flutter of Alice's hair, floating out in all directions and spangled from the sun above. I reminded myself that I could not guess all the reasons a person might say a thing so poorly, and I remembered the tenderness that presented itself when I'd pinned the brooch on Alice's collar. When I kicked back up to the surface, it was toward that feeling, to take it in my hands.

But as I wiped the water from my eyes, I saw that Alice was now uncertain. She got out of the reservoir and put her slip back on. I also got out but didn't fuss over clothes, only reached into my sack and held up a sweet mandarin. We sat down together, and she watched my fingers as I peeled it gently into one long strip of orange. I gave the naked fruit to her and she split it down the middle and gave me half. I pulled another mandarin from the bag and we ate that too, and after that another.

We didn't speak, the only sound a rising buzz of insects as the day grew hotter. My limbs stilled and grew heavy in the heat, but Alice jiggled her knees up and down, bursting out with short spurts of conversation that weighed against the beauty of our silence. I let her words fall without trying to lift them up, because I saw how she was flickering inside, and I could be patient.

At last she quieted. She stared at me as if trying to decide. Then she stood and pulled her slip off over her head so that there was nothing covering her at all. I also stood. There we were, under the sun. She smiled fleetingly as if to please me. But I did not want false expressions of pleasure, and so I waited. She turned her head and looked at the land all around and beyond me—the sage and mesquite, the rabbits scattering across the red dirt—and finally up at the sky, its deep wide blue. A slight breeze cooled us.

At last she looked back at me. A muscle rippled near her collarbone as if a small animal were loose inside her, and I touched the place to soothe it. She stepped forward and put her naked self against my own. I did not turn my eyes away from her.

Afterward we unwrapped the cornbread and pulled the jar of milk from the mud. Under the willow tree our feet tangled together like pale fish and we laughed at the sight of them. We helped each other with our clothes, and once back in her dress she was shyer than without it. I watched her walk away through sagebrush glowing purple in the late sun. Glancing down, I saw that she had buttoned my shirt up wrong but I didn't care to correct it, only whistled all the way to my pickup.

The important things are often bodiless. To render into the world a thing with no material qualities is a trick that requires bravery and luck, and is akin to art, which in the making can be uncertain and uncomfortable but in other moments sublime. At that time Alice was whole in her mind and was so for four years more.

WE HAD MANY OUTDOOR TIMES. Often we arranged to meet overnight along her walks, and I drove ahead to set up camp, a fire and supper warmed from a can and potatoes wrapped in foil, two bedrolls laid out as one but never a tent because she would not have it. Always she arrived dusty and smiling, ate all the supper and combed her hair in the pickup's rearview mirror. At night by the campfire I coaxed her into singing, and like Ma Binney she could sing fiercely, which I had not expected; but also she could sing another way, which was in a tender vein. In most ways she was either very strong or very soft, and I have never known a person with so little of anything in between.

In the mornings she set off walking for home, and once there she never sang at all. I could not understand it, this endless desire to return to such a place. I did not see why we would not go on camping forever. But it's true that over time what exists is no longer that which was first created. Though I love the old things about Alice, why hide them? It would be like hiding my own self. I love the crepe at her knee and elbow, the growing softness at her waist, her voice gone veil and shadow. Her hair is now gray at the roots but artificial brown in the length, a bid for youth that signals her regret at growing old, or perhaps other people's regret at her growing old. She lays her beautiful neck on the edge of the sink and submits to it. These attempts to mollify other people exasperate me. She is not afraid to assert herself to do the useless things that others think she should. It is the assertion of personal, more important things that stump her from time to time.

In old family photographs she is never alone. There is no record of her entire self without a part of it obscured by the parts of others. And now these people, these people who have loved her longest, they are conspiring against her! They believe her change is a diminishing, and they are afraid of it. They want to forget who she has become and remember only who she has been, and that is not a thing I believe in.

It is not possible to solve every problem. But some solutions are obvious. For example the problem of Alice's house, which lately is falling down around her. The roof flakes, the porch sags. Inside is a terrible clutter, dirty towels and stacks of old magazines, which makes it difficult to breathe and painful to think. I don't say these things to hurt her feelings, but the fact is that her house is made of little more than rotting tar paper and only the occasional wood beam.

Whereas my house up on Mesa Portales is a real and solid construction, every adobe brick mixed and made by me. My house looks west out over a canyon that although far from any ocean whatsoever yet resembles one in scope and light. This ocean canyon heaves waves of shale and basalt, quartz and silt. Cloud shadows flit across its rock floor like ghost boats.

There is no other place on Earth like Mesa Portales. I have traveled to many places, so mine is not an uninformed opinion. The truth is that there is a hierarchy. Some places are objectively better, just as some people are objectively better than others. I want to bring an objectively better person to an objectively better place. I want to bring Alice to Mesa Portales.

When I told my gallerist Fitz that I planned to move her up there with me, he was aghast. How will you do any work? You don't like people.

But I haven't done any work for some time now, and maybe for the first time I need the company more.

Alice knows it is right that she should go to Mesa Portales with me. She knows this. She nods her head when I make it all clear to her. Yet she will not go!

No, she says, because what will happen to Lorna?

It is utterly strange to me when a person recognizes what is right and yet refuses to heed it. I myself find it easy to go along with what is right, once one can divine its direction. It is freeing and releases one from all sorts of obligations that might otherwise drag one down. But not everyone sees things as clearly as I do, and so I have devised a solution to the problem of Lorna.

This solution is unusual, also irregular. But who are we if not irregular people?

Yesterday I chose an hour very dear to me, summer afternoon. Alice rested in the chair facing Lorna's grave. I sat down next to her.

Alice, I said.

I took her hand.

Alice.

She turned her lovely eyes to me.

I explained it so she would understand. I included important details: my pickup's flatbed, my strong arms and sturdy shovel, the perfect spot not far from the ledge at Mesa Portales, so that Lorna will still be near.

Come live with me and be my love, I said. No one will think it of us two old birds.

She smiled and squeezed my hand.

I squeezed her hand in return, relieved.

Yet again she shook her head! No, she said, because what will happen to Lorna?

Always her mind loops back to the problem of Lorna, which she views as irrevocable. And it's true that in the most important way the problem is irrevocable, no matter how many wild violets Alice plants in hopes of their roots reaching down to Lorna's heart. But anyone would agree that sometimes we must do things for the people we love, even when they don't understand and even when they argue against us.

2

B UT THE DIFFICULTIES, THEY BEGIN immediately.

The sun is up. I rub lard into my blistered palms. The cat crawls out from underneath Alice's bed for its dish of food, and I listen to its soft chewing. I slide the shovel underneath the bureau, all the way to the wall and just in time, because outside Frank Jr. is parking his pickup across the cattle guard as if to block me from leaving. As if I were afraid of him.

People say that Frank Jr. is trying to do right by Alice, but I see him for what he is: a dog hounding, a vulture circling. What makes him think he can take things from her, why does he expect anything at all? Why, because I am his mother, Alice always says, and smiles as if at a lovely thought.

Lately Frank Jr. has taken to hanging around the music hall in Lindrith, boasting about sitting in with musicians who pass through there. He has put it about that he'd leave town and go make records of his own if only he had the cash to make a start. On more than one occasion I've thought to give him money myself just to be rid of him, but I don't like to help a weakling. It is a bad bet, and no good can come of it.

Now he walks toward the house, spitting out his chaw at the weeping willow. Near the porch he eases his hand through the pink hollyhocks, the star-white daisies, the purple cosmos. It's a murky thing I feel, watching him be tender with Alice's flowers.

I wait at the screen door. At first Frank Jr. doesn't notice me through the wire mesh, though my nose is only a few inches from it. That is what eyes do: they focus on the front plane and so there's a delay in seeing the deeper layer. In this case the deeper layer is me, standing silently in the darkened house.

Jesus Christ, Agatha, he says when his eyes adjust. Why didn't you say anything?

We glare at each other through the wire screen, snagged all over by that imp of a cat. Alice only ever chuckles when it leaps up and hangs from the screen door, its yowls so like a piteous baby that she hurries to let it in, which does nothing to break its bad habit. Frank Jr. tries to open the door, but I've hooked the latch from the inside.

Your mother headed out on a walk not ten minutes ago, I say.

He squints at me. I don't believe you.

I unhook the latch. Look for yourself.

I feel the house sharpen as he comes in. Everything is ready, on alert, and the sun beats in through the east windows.

Ma! Frank Jr. searches behind doors and in corners and closets as if to catch me in a lie. It's a nice place I'm taking her, he shouts from the kitchen, better than this dump! They'll wait on her hand and foot; they'll make sure she doesn't wander off. There's a lady in town what will come to do her hair.

He opens the back door and looks out at the yard. Lorna's cross is still in shade, and his eyes pass right over it.

Maybe she's hiding in the chicken coop, I say. Be sure to check the compost heap.

He slams the door without going outside and turns on me. Why in hell didn't you stop her from wandering around on her own?

She's not a child, I say. Anyway, she doesn't want to see you.

He smirks. She always wants to see me.

This is unfortunately true. Whereas I never want to see him, and he feels the same about me. Just last spring he ransacked the place looking for the property deed and found the letters in Alice's desk drawer instead. These letters between Alice and me began soon after the reservoir, and often we wrote things that we did not otherwise have the voice for. Frank Jr. seized upon my opening letter, and at first it was my penmanship that bothered him most. It's the same as a man's! he said, and read the beginning out loud in a high falsetto, as if a womanly tone would shame me. *Dear Alice, thank you for your hospitality it was lovely, your company, your flowers, though you should know that the bronze zinnias are wrong next to the purple snapdragons.*

But very quickly Frank Jr.'s face sharpened. He's not a dim man. He recognized that in my handwriting is a secret he can't or won't comprehend.

I bellowed as I fought to get the letters from him. He's strong, younger than me by more than thirty years, but I would not have him read more or hear his mocking turn to disbelief and finally to anger. I was not afraid for myself, but I was afraid for Alice.

In the end he put the letters down because Alice came into the room and put her hands over her eyes as if to murder the view of us entirely. I don't begrudge anyone their due, and so when Frank Jr. hesitated at her dismay, I felt a twinge of approval at his concern for her. Nonetheless I took the opportunity to dump the hot water from the teakettle onto his bare forearm.

He hollered, and Alice's hands flew off her face. She rushed to him. Can you get some ice? she asked me. Scuffling in the house is never a good idea, oh dear.

Before obliging I gave Frank Jr. a thin, satisfied smile. His eyes were full of fury; they promised to pay me back.

Well, so what. Why should it be like air to him that he have his way?

Without hurry I took a knife from the drawer and chipped a pile of chunks off the ice block in the freezer. I arranged these frozen jewels on the blue-striped grid of a dish towel and thought what a pity that this effort would be wasted on Frank Jr. But Alice had asked it of me, and so I tied the dish towel's corners up over the ice and handed it to her. She pressed it onto Frank Jr.'s arm, crooned over him as if he were the damn cat.

I picked up the letters that had dropped from his hand when I scalded him. I'll put these back, I said. Instead I let the sound of the drawer opening and shutting stand in for doing just that. Also I dropped the deed for the house behind the desk, into a gap between the floor and the wall, where it wouldn't be found.

I thought about letting the letters melt away in the creek or burn up with the trash. But instead the next day I went to Santa Fe and stopped by my gallery so they could direct me to the correct shop for buying a purse. This request made Fitz tuck his pen behind his ear, astonished. It *was* surprising: me, Agatha Smithson, wanting a purse.

But really what I wanted was a vessel.

Fitz scratched his head and stood up. Follow me, Agatha.

So I did, up San Francisco Street to the Plaza, but as we continued on I began to agitate in my mind, because I'm not ladies' sundries. If he brought me to that sort of place I'd have to fire him, it would indicate such a fundamental misunderstanding between us. But in the end Fitz held open the door of a trading post and led me to a wall hung with leather pouches, one of which was perfect, a soft caramel leather beaded in sky blue and brick red. That's where I keep the letters now, though the strap is tight around my middle because my waist has advanced along with the years, and the purse edges up toward my armpit in the wearing of it.

Frank Jr. has a thought. What're you doing here so early anyway?

I'm helping pack your mother's things, I say. She's moving up to Mesa Portales with me.

No, he says. She's going to the place in Taos.

No, I say. She prefers Mesa Portales.

She doesn't know what she prefers, he says. Hell, she doesn't know what year it is! You heard about what happened at the post office? She accused the mail truck driver from Bernalillo of stealing that cane she's always on about. Ilona had to come out from behind the counter to reason with her. It was a Saturday, the whole town saw it! They think I'm not taking care of her.

Gossip, I say.

Face facts, Agatha! He makes a sound that starts out a laugh and ends up a sob. Ma isn't right in the head anymore. Anyway, you're not family and it's not your business.

It is my business, I say. I am the one who cares for her.

His eyes narrow. Tell me where she went to.

I shrug. Most days she enjoys a walk to her childhood home, I say.

That much is true. Of course she doesn't find her family there and on occasion it is necessary to remind her that all of that was long ago. But this is only natural. In some moments a person is who she has always been, and in others she is a new person entirely. There is no reason to make a fuss or put a stop to it.

I'll be back later and I don't want to see you here, Frank Jr. says. His face grows sly with a secret. And you better wait to hear from my lawyer before making any plans about Mesa Portales.

I'm startled but won't let him take my own breath away from me and puff himself up with it.

I don't wait on other people to make my plans, I say.

He grins. One of his front teeth is black at the edges. He steps back out onto the porch, spits his chaw into the roses, and heads toward his pickup. This time he ignores the flowers but slows his steps past the willow tree. Alice has told me about the hideaway he and Lorna made for themselves beneath its branches when they were small, how summers they played all day and slept out there on tiny bedrolls, and Alice brought them supper on plates with yellow roses painted around the edges. All this when her husband was gone on hunting trips, because he was not one for pampering his children, even if Alice was. Once I found Alice and Frank Jr. laughing, their hands clasped across the kitchen table, and when they turned their faces toward me and smiled their identical smiles, I had an unhappy feeling.

Now Frank Jr. squats and ducks his head underneath the cascade of branches. He stays there, looking, before getting back in his pickup and driving away.

ONCE HE'S GONE I WASH the coffee cups and set them on the dish towel to dry. I marvel at the curve of each cup's handle, the rough weave of the dish towel, the iridescence of suds lingering in the sink. Everything is new and beautiful and strange, and my hands tremble.

I remind myself to think clearly. I wind the clock on the fireplace mantel and arrange a quilt on the couch. I tidy the magazine pile but leave *Good Housekeeping* open on the side table. Last I toss an apple core and a pile of carrot tops into an old Folgers coffee can and carry it outside to the compost heap.

The coyote skulks near the lilacs. It often comes around because Alice has taken to tossing it leftover bones. I've reminded her over and over about rabies, but still she calls and coos to the coyote because she no longer reliably recognizes what is a danger to her. For example in the compost is a rattlesnake I killed with the hoe three days ago. I'd chopped it at the neck, neatly and cleanly, but Alice cried as the headless body thrashed because she had forgotten its venom and imagined I'd killed a poor, defenseless creature.

I shout at the coyote; it scrabbles over the adobe wall and disappears. Then I sit on the back porch in the shade, where I have never sat before, and watch the light move across the yard until Lorna's grave is lit with full sun and I can consider it carefully.

But my eyes are drawn to the lilac bushes, whose leaves have begun to droop long before the hottest time of day. It is upsetting to see these lilacs falter. In spring Alice often cuts me a flowering branch and lodges it in a jar of water that I tuck between my thighs to steady on the drive back to Mesa Portales. I always leave the cut branch loose on the ledge for the wind and pour the water from the jar into my rainwater barrel, so as not to waste it.

It is finally the memory of Frank Jr.'s voice that rouses me: *And you better wait to hear from my lawyer before making any plans about Mesa Portales.*

Before I go, I inspect the yard. Here is the shed, here is the vegetable garden, here are the potted geraniums on the back porch. There is Lorna's grave. Nothing different or unusual can be seen, not by anyone, not even by me.

3

W**HEN I FIRST CAME TO** New Mexico fifteen years ago, the wide-open sky was a great permission to me. Also the beauty was painful and I wasn't prepared for it.

My friend had been offered a position at a university in Albuquerque but said there was nowhere like New York and he would never leave it. After many difficult years he had recently found success, including museum exhibitions and acquisitions by collectors. So when the university came calling, he suggested, How about Agatha Smithson, a real up-and-comer!

We laughed over that, a little bitterly, but laughter of any kind whatsoever was welcome, as this was soon after Bellevue, a terrible place I woke to find myself in. There were many days I could not account for. My friend said that I had burned my canvases and behaved badly at various events, and also that these things had frightened Masha's child. I was fond of Masha's child, who lived upstairs and came to my studio after school. This child felt no need for talk but only ate an apple or piece of bread and read a book in my chair until Masha came home. In winter I followed the two of them upstairs to sleep with Masha, who had a small heater powered by an extension cord run over from the next building. Sometimes she sought me out under the heavy quilts that pinned us to the bed, but at that time the river inside me was frozen. Later I understood that the city's energies were not my own: the manicured parks, the bouquets atop tables and corsages pinned to collars, the lipsticked petals of women's mouths as they brushed past me on the street—these were pallid substitutes, and I could not be warmed by them.

I didn't remember frightening Masha's child but I was sorry over it. The only frightened face that rose up dimly in my memory from that time was Julien's. I have never told anyone that I suspect Julien was the reason I ended up at Bellevue. He was afraid of my changing. I have never forgotten it.

When my friend told me these things, I was wearing a hospital gown and sat in a hospital chair next to a hospital bed. His eyes were bright and sharp, while at that time my own were dim and watery. I had no reason to doubt him. You must try to get better, he said to me.

I am a strong person, no one would say otherwise, and though it's true that strong or not strong is often beside the point in these matters, I took my friend's advice and in the end came back to myself. But while I was at Bellevue my building had been demolished and all the artists evicted. I had no place to live or to work, though that did not bother me as much as everyone imagined, because I did not plan to ever paint again. At that time I had no enthusiasm for any part of life. So I shrugged at the mention of a university position.

But my friend—who now had a loft farther uptown with electricity and hot water, and wore a new wool overcoat—gripped my shoulders. Agatha, he said, you need the salary and the faculty housing. You need the fresh start.

He organized a farewell party in my honor, which I protested because I did not care for good-byes and also felt shame about Bellevue. But my friend waved off my wishes. He said that the party was not only for me but also for other people—*your friends, Agatha*—and that he would not accept declarations of timidity or shame because he did not believe in them in regard to me.

He bought me a new shirt and trousers, and also gave me his dove-gray flannel jacket, which I had long admired. In the pocket of the jacket I found a cream linen handkerchief with purple pansies embroidered in one corner. At the party I gave this handkerchief to Masha's child, who accepted it with dignity, then helped collect money for my bus ticket and brought it to me afterward in an old knit cap, weighted down by coins.

The only person I did not see at this party was Julien. But my friend said he had never met anyone by the name of Julien and so could not have known to invite him.

The next morning my friend accompanied me to Port Authority, which in fact had been where we first met, arriving to the city on the same day and striking up a conversation on a bench just outside the terminal. He led me to that bench and said, What a long way we've come.

On that first day in the city, we'd met his cousin on a stoop and followed her up five flights of stairs. For that climb I expected something grand, but it wasn't, not until in the kitchen I beheld a wall covered with copper jelly molds shaped like horseshoes and hearts, fish and flowers and birds, all on hooks in a large, rectangular pegboard. The molds were hung curve to crook alongside one another like a gleaming puzzle, and the cousin had not made one mistake in the arrangement of them.

This cousin insisted that we bathe and afterward threw out the brush we'd scrubbed with. At night she gave me the bed and herself the chair by the window, while my friend slept on the sofa in the next room. You stay over there, she said, and raised a finger warningly, but I knew it was for show and that she was not afraid of me. She slept with her hands tucked under her cheek and in the morning got up without a lazy instant. I pretended sleep as she pulled on black stockings and pressed beeswax into her cracked hands. Then she went out the door and I never saw her again, as my friend and I moved on to other circles.

My friend had shown me how to mix paint and stretch a canvas, and insisted I go see many things: paintings and photographs and sculptures, sometimes a lecture at a museum; and once, best of all, in the dim corner of a *Wunderkammer*, a fish-man no bigger than my hand, suspended on a wire and swimming in the air, its tiny skull atop a skeleton chest that gave way to the bones of its fish tail.

As we waited for the bus that would put New York behind me, he gave advice, as he had once been a teacher in Missouri. Anything you say, he said, the students will write it down. Just say a thing and watch as they write, the sequence of these two actions will fortify you.

I told him I didn't rely on the actions of others to fortify me, and he laughed until he cried, waved good-bye as the bus pulled away. It is easier to have friends in youth, we are more open and understanding to each other. He made me promise to stay in touch, but I am a person who always moves forward. I have since regretted this quality in myself, as my friend died years later without my having been in touch at all; and I have never cared to visit New York again because of this failure of mine.

VERY SOON AT THE UNIVERSITY in Albuquerque there were complaints. The department head was unhappy because entire class periods passed without a word uttered by me. The students shifted in their seats and waved their hands in the air to get my attention. This pained me, as my mother had often refused to speak to me for weeks at a time and for reasons I could not decipher, and I did not want to inflict a similar misery. But a dreadful weight pressed down and I could not rouse myself. In this way perhaps I understood my mother for the first time.

At night I stared up at the sky and tried to see into the emptiness between the stars, but if this went on too long I felt strange and not myself. One evening my neighbor Dan, a graduate student, leaned over the patio fence and offered me a cigarette. I'd never cared for smoking, but I accepted the cigarette because Dan's voice was kind and because I had become afraid of where my thoughts might lead me. Dan lit a cigarette for himself also, and I enjoyed our evening very much; in fact this habit revived and sustained me for years afterward. At the university I became a wonderful smoker, there was no one better at it than me. Though when I moved to Mesa Portales I gave it up without a second thought, as there is no point in smoking alone.

Dan was twenty-four when we met. He is a creative person but ruled by intellect, and so I approved of his choice of the architecture program. After graduation he worked, he won a few awards, and later I recommended him for a faculty position. When he married, I didn't worry. Melinda is a fine person, though without exceptional qualities. By his account she is a wonderful wife and mother, and I'm happy he has her because she frees him for more important things. Yet I have not seen him in recent months.

Back then Dan sat and smoked with me for hours. He did not care if I spoke or not, though after some time I did speak, and when he asked gentle questions I told him about Ma Binney and Bellevue, about how I had not yet painted anything worth the time it took to do it. When I said that the vastness of the sky in this place frightened me, he touched my shoulder and said, Only a fool wouldn't be frightened. Slowly I grew accustomed to it and remembered that it was also the sky from my childhood.

After some weeks I felt inside myself a suggestion. I drew four horizontal lines on the classroom blackboard, one below the other. After that I sat among the students. They scooted their chairs to be closer to me, and we all of us together looked at the lines on the chalkboard and tried to see. The students relaxed their eyes. I also relaxed.

Every day after that I drew the lines. The students would gather around and console me with their animal closeness. They breathed so unceasingly and with such confidence! They coughed and sniffled; they sighed and shuffled their feet. Also they took up smoking along with me, and these communal noises and gestures—the scratch of the match and the brief hot flare, the inhales and the exhales, the stubbing out of ash, all of us together—all these things were wonderful. One student, a potter, brought in a large ceramic ashtray, yellow with white markings, and by the end of every class it was overflowing. Yet each new class period it was empty and clean, and this was also wonderful.

In the beginning these lines I drew were only an impulse and a reason to sit among my students. But when I began to work outside the classroom, I added vertical lines to form a grid, and this was the beginning of the work that made my name.

It was a strange thing to have a name. It grew and grew, and sometimes I wondered what it might conjure up, if Ma Binney would see this name of mine and appear with all her widows to see my paintings hung on a gallery wall. She would not think much of them because they did not resemble anything that she saw in the world, and she would suspect high-handedness.

But the department chair knew an important thing when it was in front of him, and especially after *Art in America* there was never again a bother over my teaching practices. I began to speak in class about ways to see and look and how to roll a cigarette properly, about the wanderings of my youth. My classes were popular. Over the years I had exhibitions in Berlin, Miami, Copenhagen, Milan. I did not miss New York.

But after nearly a decade I felt the old darkness. I had recently gone back to Saskatchewan to find my family, but the town had dwindled and disappeared and any news of my family with it. No one knew them and no one could locate them, not even the private detective that Dan hired for me. It was as if this family of mine had never been. As that was the way I had lived since running away from home, it felt to me as though I had murdered them with my indifference. A feeling of regret and sorrow settled inside me, a poisonous smoke that at times grew so thick I was unable to breathe. I recognized this smoke: it had been in the air right before Bellevue, and now it had blown back my way.

But this time I knew better than to stay where people might

misunderstand. I don't care to ever wake up in a hospital ward again. I packed my things and I left Albuquerque, though every spring Dan arranges for me to return and give a guest lecture at the university. On these occasions a fuss is made over me, and I enjoy it very much.

I DROVE NORTH AND WEST away from the university. In the beginning I camped. Later I asked a gas station owner, a man with a white mustache and shirt buttons pulled askew by the fat of his waist, Is there any land for lease? Away from other people, higher up, with a view.

This man, who was Alice's husband, looked me up and down. It's not from desire that people look, but because they think me strange. I am not bothered. He said that in fact his wife had ninety acres up at Mesa Portales as part of a family inheritance, and perhaps an arrangement could be made. He jotted down directions and told me to come back if I was interested. If so we could sign a lease at the lawyer's office.

I drove to Mesa Portales straightaway. It was fifteen miles from town, and the road was rough and slow. At one point I made a wrong turn down an arroyo that in deep summer had wildflowers sprouting from its craggy walls. I followed it a quarter mile before backing up to the road and trying again.

By the time I got to the top of Mesa Portales the sun was setting. I hustled to the rock ledge and saw the ocean canyon for the first time. Immediately I understood that at Mesa Portales the rock is alive, that a person can feel the forces behind things that at other times they take for granted. I felt a loosening in my chest. The smoke cleared out of it and disappeared into the ocean canyon. In its wake a clean silence remained. I knew that this would be a place where I could work.

In the near distance a prickly pear rooted into the sandstone, a spiny tooth in a rock maw. I parked my pickup near the ledge and slept in the back with the tailgate down so I could see the view, and at night the ocean canyon became a shifting emptiness stretching out to an invisible horizon.

In the morning I drove back to the gas station and told Alice's husband I would sign his papers. I saw by the way he eyed me closely and tucked his pencil behind his ear that he had been calculating figures, wondering how much he could get away with charging me. But I understood that he was a small man. Whatever figure he came up with would be small to me, just like he was.

He squinted at me. What's your line of work? Housepainter, that kind of thing?

I was wearing overalls. There was paint on them. Sure, I said.

I was the first to arrive at his lawyer's office. This office was painted a dirty blue without good qualities. It stank of damp feed, and in fact chickens pecked the ground outside the office window. Also there was a large, round clock mounted above the outside front door, its black electrical cord snaking along the porch to a jury-rigged outlet. This was nothing less than an unwanted knock on the door of one's life, as any time of day or night that a person glanced at the place, they were forced to know the hour, whether they cared to or not.

Why did you put this clock on the outside of your house? I asked as we waited.

So everyone knows what time it is. The chicken-lawyer said this as if it were obvious. Consider it a public service, you can take a look as you drive by.

It's hideous in every way, I told him. I meant this both philosophically and aesthetically.

Folks around here are used to it, he said. But you're not from here.

That clock has got neon lights.

That's right, he said, proud.

I didn't tell him that the green and red lights emitting from the clockface were wrong with the dirty blue of his house and that it hurt me to see this. So the last few minutes of my life before I met Alice were spent fretting about the grotesque misplacement of this clock and the suffering it brought to anyone who saw it without even knowing its effect.

Then Alice walked through the door. Her husband led her in as if he were the one in charge, as it turned out he was. Everything about her was delicate and awkward and wary, like a colt that had managed to stay a colt all the way to sixty-one years without life imposing too much upon it. At least that was my impression in those first moments.

Alice wore a sky-blue jersey pantsuit and a white shirt with a round collar. Lorna's thunderbird brooch was pinned crookedly on the lapel; I yearned to straighten it for her. Overall she was lively, bright, like a bird. She had a chatty way of moving through the room, thanking everyone right and left and overmuch, and I saw that she used her politeness to create distance between herself and whichever man she spoke to. To my surprise I found I regarded her fondly straight from the beginning.

Here's the lady what-that I was telling you about, Alice's husband said to her. He had a habit of using *what-that*. At first I thought it was local slang, but it turned out to be his phrase alone. He was his own country, one it was a tragedy to visit.

Alice turned to look at me. Her eyes are mild and run-of-the-mill hazel. I find them one of her strongest attractions. She took my sturdy hand in her bird-bone one and stared at me frankly.

I know what she saw: a woman her own age, more than sixtyish, thick around the middle, in denim overalls and a button-down shirt, the top button of which I had done up for the occasion. My hair is gray, cropped short. I smiled at her, because how could I not? She was about to grant me a new home. I saw she had warm feelings in return, but they were the generalized sort that she has for most humans and all animals, and at that time had nothing to do with me in particular.

I was given only one option, a lifetime lease, which I immediately accepted at the terms offered. The husband and the chicken-lawyer exchanged smirks because they thought I was a foolish woman who didn't know she was being had. But I am an artist, and I have plenty of money from being one. They were the fools, to lease away such a place. If they think I'll die early, they are mistaken.

First the chicken-lawyer indicated that I should sign on a certain line, the beginning of which he marked with an X so like a chicken scratch that I laughed out loud. He was startled. Is anything amiss?

Not at all, I said, and signed my name quickly because I wanted the land and the lease and no problems. I stood as I signed because I did not care to sit.

Next the chicken-lawyer waved his hand to indicate that it was Alice's turn. She sat down in the chair and signed where they told her to. My intentions toward the deal that was occurring were pure, as I wanted a home and was willing to pay a fair price for it; and yet I felt a difficulty in my chest, as I did not like how they said what she was to do and how she then did do it. The men laughed together, their breath heavy and foul-smelling, and suddenly there were too many people in the room for my liking, it felt hot and close, and I noticed that somehow in this arid country the walls were damp with stains.

But Alice smiled at me and said she hoped I would be happy there. She said that Mesa Portales had been a favorite of hers to hike up to in her younger days.

You're welcome to come for the view whenever you like, I said.

In fact I wanted no person to ever come up for the view or for anything else at all. I only wanted to work my paints and my problems. And yet I spoke those words not five minutes after meeting Alice. But at that time I was not fit for anyone, and I made sure to forget about her promptly.

Afterward I took a square of old plywood and made a *No Trespassing* sign lettered in burnt orange so that it could not be missed. Then I drove to Mesa Portales, and at the property line I nailed the sign to the gatepost. I lifted the wire loop off the gate and opened it, drove through, then closed the gate behind me. These actions filled me with a peace that before I'd felt only after a long stretch of work.

I had nothing to back up the *No Trespassing* sign if anyone ignored it and came up to bother me, nothing except myself. My friend Josey asked me, didn't I want a dog? If he'd been a grown man I would've thought he meant that I should have a dog for protection, but because he was seven at the time I knew he meant did I want one for love. Maybe I did want a dog for love, but I wasn't going to have one. At that time I did not want a creature that needed me or that I grew to need.

4

'D FIRST MET JOSEY WHEN I was out driving for the early-morning pleasure of it, not long after the occasion of the lifetime lease. On the road I saw a person walking, a child. I slowed down and asked, did he want a ride? Josey got in next to me without a word. We've been pals six years now.

Josey might have imagined that a grown woman who lived many years in New York City would overpay for help building a mud house on top of a mesa, but I don't believe in paying a young person more than they are due. They will come to expect everything for nothing.

To begin we loaded empty barrels into the pickup. We filled them with water from the creek and brought the barrels back up the mesa to make the bricks. Josey argued that this was unnecessary. We could mix the bricks near the creek, he said, line them up on boards, and let them dry right there on the creek bank. No one was about and no one would care, and no one would steal our bricks because it was cinder blocks that everyone wanted now anyway.

But that's not what I wanted. It didn't have to be easy. Easy wasn't the point. The point was to do it so that it felt right. What do you mean by it feels right? Josey asked, grumpy. The sun was hot and strong, and he had no hat to shade his face. I thought about giving him mine, but I was the older person, after all, the one most likely to get sunstroke.

The bricks must be mixed with the air up on the mesa, I said, not the air down by the creek.

What's wrong with the creek air?

It's not what I want. That's all.

Josey's uncle Felix came in his truck with a load of wooden frames for the bricks. Why don't you build your house at the bottom of the mesa where you can get some cover, Uncle Felix said as he squinted out over the ocean canyon. It's going to be hot or cold up here, one way or the other, most all the time.

Josey waited for what I would say next, which was nothing, not a word. Instead I began laying out the wooden frames end to end, north to south, and by the time I finished, Uncle Felix was gone.

I outlined the house in the dirt with a stick. It would be a large room, with an easel for working on one end, a table in the middle, and a low wall marking out the space for sleeping on the other. Also I had firm ideas that could not be brooked as regards the windows, in order that the light fall properly. In fact I took care to match the windows in Georgia's studio, large-paned and on the north wall, an arrangement I had often admired while visiting with her. I first met Georgia years ago when I went to Ghost Ranch to thank her for her paintings, which show the truth that exists between the things inside us and the things outside us. I did not add that from looking at her work I had also understood how to go beyond what she had done.

But perhaps she suspected that, because at first she looked at me hard without saying a word. Then she laughed and invited me in for lunch, and that is how we began.

I have always known on the canvas what is true and what is not, and I require no advice in this regard. But talking things over with Georgia has often been clarifying to me. Sometimes she says a thing that strikes me right or offers thoughts that I have not considered. Most important, we share the view that among the worst of crimes is to take a foolish idea and dress it up in beauty so that the banal things of life and thought are glorified. There is nothing so abhorrent as sentimentality.

In the beginning Georgia and I talked of traveling together on freight ships, a kind of adventure, possibly to Manila and Hong Kong and Singapore, until it seemed to me that such a trip might actually transpire if we kept on discussing it. Then I had to stop that talk, to say that traveling was not for me, though of course I do travel to all kinds of places, because once people see my work they also want to see me. But traveling with Georgia would be too distracting, too stimulating. In fact Georgia talks so much and so well that sometimes after a visit with her I drive away, out of sight of her house, and pull over to nap in the car before I am able to continue on.

But now Georgia and I are no longer friends, and I must rely on myself. I take care not to be sentimental about her. At one time I had an exhibition poster from her Whitney retrospective pinned up on the wall, but I was afraid things would be taken from me in so much looking, and so I took it down. On occasion I am subject to doubts, and it is important to set yourself apart from them whenever possible.

TO BEGIN, JOSEY AND I dug out the floor, and after that we mixed mud with straw, filled the brick forms, and left them to bake in the sun. I intended to begin building the walls as soon as each set of bricks dried, but Josey had a different idea in his head. Instead he took those first bricks out of the forms and lined them up on the ground in even rows that stretched toward the edge of the mesa.

I am not one to let a person decide anything for me, but he did not wait for me to agree, and very quickly I understood that he was right in what he did. He started a second row, a third. After that we continued in this way, with bricks for more than a hundred orderly feet in every direction. We left a slim strip for walking between the house and the pickup, and also allowed for a path to the ledge overlooking the ocean canyon.

It was late summer before the making and laying out of bricks was complete. On that day we walked the perimeter of the grid of bricks, and as we did the geometry shifted, the rows fracturing and reordering, over and over, in a constantly changing but harmonious repetition. Josey began to laugh. I knew why he was laughing, though likely he did not. He was laughing with joy because this was the moment when the house was perfect. I knew that moment wouldn't last, and I slowed our progress so that he could relish it. Then each day the light grew sharper, my bedroll could no longer ward off the chill of early mornings at Mesa Portales, and the feel of autumn urged me on to finish.

Weekends Dan drove out to help. He brought peanut butter and tomatoes and sliced white bread, a cooler with ice cream in a tub and chocolate syrup in a can, and also beer, which we let Josey share because after all he was doing the work of a man. On one occasion Dan brought his camera to document the array of bricks, but I forbade him to use it. That is the sort of thing the land art people do, some of whom can never so much as hoist a shovel without trumpeting it all about. I don't believe in photographs except on rare occasions, because they are a decoy and a killer of true memory. Anyway, people long before us built things here, old foundations in protected valleys, cliff caves shored up with mud bricks. There is no reason to crow over a thing one has not invented.

We set the vigas in early fall, and Dan insisted on being slow and thorough with the roof. There is a leak in one spot, but this matters only in August when the thunderstorms arrive, and in any case there is always a bucket handy.

WHEN THE HOUSE WAS FINISHED there was a spell of unusually hot weather. People said that in the next town over a rancher combusted up at high noon and transformed into a shrieking ball of fire on a day thereby proved too hot for living. But at night on Mesa Portales the thin air chilled under the blue-black spangle of sky.

Josey and I lay on the rock ledge and let its leftover heat seep into us. I told him to forget what anyone said about the patterns in the sky, dippers big and little, warriors with belts and swords. There is no order to the stars, only the arrangements that people have conjured here and there for comfort.

He told me about his favorite game, which begins by stealing a crate of bottles from the grange hall. At dusk he and his friends lug the crate down into a nearby box canyon and leave the crate at the foot of the cliff wall. After that they spend time shoving each other for fun or throwing matches on the ground, and when sparks light up its dry grasses they whoop and stomp out the flames. Later, when the night is pitch-black, they draw straws. The loser kicks over the crate of bottles to make a glassy racket, then begins counting, *One, two, three, four . . .* The others scrabble up the cliff wall, scattering wide and clinging where they can, disappearing into the dark.

At fifty the boy stops counting and pulls a bottle from the pile. He yells the warning: *Bottle!* Everyone freezes. A deep silence comes over the canyon as the boy with the bottle winds his arm back to throw— and everyone holds their breath and listens for the bottle to smash on the canyon wall.

It's the best game I've ever played, Josey said. Someone gets hit by a bottle, or they don't.

He had discovered that a thing can be beautiful and terrifying at the same time, and that a person can burst from the luxury of it. That is a wonderful game, Josey, I agreed. You are learning the important things.

Later we built a bonfire. Josey had argued against this because of the dry land and heat all around, but he could not prevail over me. I had work that I did not want in the world anymore, because I had new things in mind.

While the fire burned we circled around it and kept a sharp eye out for sparks. At the last I threw on a wooden frame, its wood rotted and cracked and no good for a new canvas. It blazed up all at once, the four sides marking out the darkness within its boundaries.

Josey was happy when the fire burned down to ashes and there had been no mishaps. We pushed sticks through slippery lengths of trout and cooked them over the coals. Afterward we worked at picking slim bones from between our teeth.

Later that night he stopped shoveling dirt on the coals. Do you hear something? he said, a spooked look on his face. Because I thought I heard a voice.

I froze. In the dark, I listened. But only the sound of the ocean canyon sounded back to me, its silty undertow. I let out my breath.

I don't hear anything, I said. For the first time in years that was true.

WHENEVER THE STACK OF PAINTINGS intrudes too far into the room, I send a note to Dan and he comes in his car. We remove the canvases from the stretchers, roll them up, and ease them into metal tubes. Dan drives the tubes to Fitz, who stores them in a room presided over by a hygrometer of brass and wood, a gorgeous instrument that I make a special stop to admire each time I go to Santa Fe.

Many of these paintings are exhibited and sold, though some will go to Dan to manage when I die, as I have appointed him my executor. Before we roll each painting, we invent a title and I scrawl it on the back of the canvas. It's kinder to give a title, Dan says. I don't agree with that as it is not a matter of kind or not kind, but Fitz also insists that they are necessary, and I can be agreeable when it is required. So we take turns choosing. *Friendship. Beauty. Tree. Joy. Cloud.* We laugh, as if these names are so simple that they are ridiculous. But deep down we know that they are not.

These paintings exist on their own and are separate from me. But it's true they could only have been made here at Mesa Portales and would not exist in the world otherwise. They resemble the ocean canyon exactly, but also not at all. Instead there are pencil lines and horizontal washes of color, imperfect along every edge; there are no signposts, there is only the act of looking. It is possible to feel outside oneself if one knows how to look beyond things. That is my scheme.

Josey comes to Mesa Portales for an hour or for a week, and I pay him the same wages I would pay a grown man, minus the room and board that I provide to him. This means inside the house if it is cold, but far more often the privilege of sleeping under the stars. I cook for him as I cook for myself. I let him wake when he wishes. Our natural rhythms dictate the day, but also I insist on work. That is the only way to make good on anything in this world.

Often now he pencils the lines on my canvases before I begin, and from the start he has done it better than anyone other than myself could do. I taught him how to make the calculations, and he is handy with the metal T square. He understands that the lines must be exact and the space between them of correct proportion, because nothing whatsoever is possible in my work if there is deviation from exactness.

Josey never pauses until he is finished, and if he makes a mistake he starts again. When he puts the T square and pencil down, I begin with my brush. I trust him entirely. It is rare that a child disappoints you; it is only older people who have that skill.

5

FROM ALICE'S HOUSE IT IS an unremarkable four miles to an unremarkable town. People don't come this way much, which is how I like it. I drive slowly and with concentration, in order to be clear in my mind about what has happened and what is still ahead. I park at the chicken-lawyer's office and avoid looking at his clock. Through the window I see dirty stockinged feet up on the desk. I bang the door open.

Agatha, the chicken-lawyer says. He swivels his chair, swings his feet to the floor, and shoves them into work boots. You've saved me a trip.

What's this about?

Well, it's a matter of your lease. Frank Jr. will be terminating the contract and proceeding with a sale of the Mesa Portales property to the Bureau of Land Management.

I have a talent for animosity and at times it radiates from me strongly. On this occasion I feel it extremely, like a flu chill.

I have a lifetime lease, I say.

He puts an envelope down on the desk and slides it toward me. This is your official notification. Copy of paperwork from the BLM regarding the sale as well. You have ten days to vacate the Mesa Portales premises, and there is no legal recourse as the lease you signed has been deemed invalid. We're making this action on Mrs. Johnson's behalf via the power of attorney, and all of that is within Frank Jr.'s purview.

Ha, I say. Haha!

He sighs. We don't much understand what you do up there on the mesa, Ms. Smithson. But whatever it is, you can do it elsewhere.

I'm not leaving, I say. Alice is moving up to Mesa Portales with me.

The chicken-lawyer shakes his head. Frank Jr. has no desire for his mother to spend her golden years in a remote location without indoor plumbing or electricity, he says. The place in Taos costs a pretty penny, and Mesa Portales must be sold in order to maintain Mrs. Johnson's happiness. Naturally Frank Jr. wishes her to be surrounded by caring people and not dependent on a stranger, a foreigner.

I am the most caring person in Alice's life, I say. I am the person to maintain her happiness. Anyhow I am Canadian, which hardly counts.

But you are foreign in other ways, he says mildly. People feel that Mrs. Johnson hasn't been as well protected as she should have been, these last years.

I feel a few things, unspeakable things, because I don't believe in taking people to task for their private pleasures. But also in this moment I remember the shovel under the bureau and remind myself that it is important to be careful.

I have never known you or anyone else in this town to present yourself on Alice's front porch to offer any kind of safety or happiness, I say. Only Frank Jr. turns up, badgering her for money.

Frank Jr. has power of attorney and it's his right to sell the property to whoever he wants, the chicken-lawyer says. Perhaps you might make him a better offer.

But I won't, because owning things is not for me and I have always avoided it. It would be an anchor, owning a place, and it is against my nature to do so.

I take the envelope off his desk. My lawyer will be in touch, I say, and believe me when I tell you that he is a New York shark. Frank Jr. must stick to the lease. You tell him to stay off the property in the meantime.

If the chicken-lawyer is rattled by talk of my shark-lawyer, he doesn't let on. In fact he puts his feet back up on the desk, and I hear him chuckle when I slam the door shut on my way out. I kick at the chickens at the bottom of the porch steps. They squawk and hop out of my reach before immediately forgetting whatever was just in their heads, a skill that is in fact a chicken's greatest gift.

THE POSTMISTRESS LETS ME HAVE the back room all to myself. On the table is a yellow phone with a notepad and pencil lined up neatly beside it. Twelve squares of sunlight shine in through the paned window and onto the table's scratched honey surface. The sharp-edged neatness of this overall arrangement soothes me. I can count on the postmistress. We are disciplined people.

I pick up the phone and call my shark-lawyer.

Gus answers right away. I can tell from the gravel in his voice that he hasn't had his first lunch martini. Damn it, Agatha! I'm headed out the door.

Listen, Gus. Listen to me.

Gus has never heard my voice waver, and I can feel his sudden and deep attention through the phone line. I explain it to him: the lease, Frank Jr., the chicken-lawyer.

All right, Gus says. What is the chicken-lawyer's actual name?

I shout and ask the postmistress, who writes it down for me.

Forward me the letter, Gus says. I'll get it squared away. Try not to fuss over it, Agatha.

Before hanging up we talk about contracts for upcoming exhibitions in Brussels and Buenos Aires, the museum and gallery details, what kind of transportation will be arranged. I prefer a student to drive me around, I say. No critics, I can't abide their talk.

I know, Gus says. He promises to be in touch soon about Mesa Portales.

I give the postmistress the chicken-lawyer's paperwork, and she puts it in a new envelope for Gus and drops it in the mailbag. I decide that I won't think about this matter again until I hear from Gus. There are so many distractions these days, also so much to do, and what use can I be to Alice if I allow them?

The postmistress offers me an apple: small, green, with a powerful crunch. She sits across the table from me and we eat in companionable silence. This apple is the most wonderful apple I've ever eaten, and the sun streams into the room, pulsing and glowing in a steady rhythm, and I take it as a sign that I am proceeding correctly.

The postmistress eats her apple entirely, including stem and seeds, and so do I. Then she wipes her hands on her pants, leans forward, and touches me on the arm. Too bad about the other day when Alice was here, she says. It's a shame how everyone around here talks. It's not her fault she gets confused now and then. People are sure hard on Frank Jr. about it.

This conversation dims the light and also ruins our lovely quiet, so instead of answering I pointedly stare out the window at the post-mistress's kitchen garden. She is partial to vegetables, allows petunias and marigolds only as a measure to ward off bugs, and arranges the plantings in a precise and pleasing formal pattern. In fact it could be said that everything about the postmistress is high yielding and well tended, a person whose hands are very clean and whose posture is very upright, and who does not waste a person's time on unnecessary talk.

But then she continues talking!

Agatha, she says, does Alice talk to you about Lorna?

I glare at her, because it is outrageous that the postmistress would imagine that Alice would not talk to me of Lorna.

But the postmistress doesn't shift her gaze. Instead she looks back at me steadily and never blinks. As I am not a person who ever looks away first, our eyes are locked until the postmistress is satisfied in some private way, perhaps the result of a very slight nod I bestow her, in an effort to throw her off her game. She nods back as if I've given the correct answer, when in fact I have given no answer at all.

All right then, she says, as if relieved. What's Alice up to today?

But some things are not the postmistress's business.

Instead I tell her what I'm doing at Mesa Portales. Right now it is the end of one thing, I say, and the beginning of another. I am building some things and destroying others. I don't tell her I am also trying to outrun things. I find it easy to speak to casual acquaintances, and the postmistress is a good listener, though now and then she opens her mouth as if to say something, then shuts it again without a word.

I notice the calm and peace of sitting with her. It gives me a feeling that might be a painting of some kind. I invite her to visit Mesa Portales, and even as those words come out of my mouth, I don't regret them. But before she can reply, a man comes in shouting for his package. There's always a man and he's always shouting. One day even Josey will turn into one.

The postmistress smiles at the man as she helps him, which irritates me. What did he do to earn her smile?

I scowl at him on my way out.

What bit you? he asks, sneering.

The postmistress calls after me, but the bloom is gone.

6

I **LEAVE THE POSTMISTRESS BEHIND.** I drive to Josey's house and honk; I keep the engine running. Josey bursts out the front door and sprints to the pickup. This is the usual way of things.

But today his mother appears in the doorway and flags me down. We rarely talk, his mother and I. Josey has told me about her new beau, who never shows up empty-handed: a sack of apples, a side of bacon, a bag of flour, or a handful of nails to fix the buckling floorboards in the kitchen. At first Josey's mother only thanked this man and sent him on his way, but one evening he coaxed them all over to Josey's father's grave, where a wooden fence now surrounded it, a fence Josey hated straight off because it made the grave stand out lonely on the valley floor. But Josey said his mother walked around the fence admiring it, and when she came back around to where the beau stood watching, she held out her hand to him.

Now Josey's mother walks over to my pickup, and I admire her dark hair, the silver hoop in each earlobe. I think of her beau with his clever courting and wonder if he deserves her.

Frank Jr. came by looking for his mother, she says. He's worried she might be out wandering lost somewhere.

I saw Alice this morning, I say. She's not lost.

That's good to hear, she says.

Frank Jr. just likes to stir the pot, I say.

She shakes her head. I went to school with him. He acts rough, but he has a good heart.

She asks me and Josey to wait a moment, then goes back into the house and returns carrying a pie tin with a checkered cloth over it. Will you take this to Mrs. Johnson? She loves a blackberry buckle. Ilona used to pick berries down by our creek to make it for her.

I take the pie tin. The postmistress?

They've been friends for years and years, she says. She was a real comfort to her when Lorna passed. You'll tell Frank Jr. you saw his mother?

I pass the pie tin over to Josey and put the pickup into gear. But Josey's mother puts a hand on the hood to stop me.

Josey needs to be home by dark, she says. We're headed to Albuquerque tomorrow to get him some new shoes.

Josey settles the blackberry buckle at his feet and stares ahead as if his mother has not spoken at all. I approve of this behavior. He should be resolved in his own life. What his mother wants should have no effect on him at all, as in this sort of relation there is a tendency for control that is wrongheaded and pretends to be based on love. But it isn't.

I watch Josey's mother in the rearview mirror as we drive away: her slim figure, hand raised to shade her face.

Listen, Josey, I say once his house and mother have disappeared behind us. Today will be a big day.

We share such a perfect understanding that he knows I mean that the hours will be long and the work will be hard, and he nods, waits for more. But I hesitate. I am reluctant to say the words out loud, what it is we are to do.

Alice and Lorna are moving to Mesa Portales, I say.

He turns to look at me. But Lorna's dead. She was shot, it was in the face, it was before I was born! His eyes bug out as if life before his own existence were but a brutal fairy tale.

You are correct, I say, and it is a terrible thing. But now Alice is moving to Mesa Portales and she won't leave Lorna behind. That is her final word on the subject.

He stares out the window. Is Lorna in a coffin? he asks.

I can't say for sure.

I don't want to see her.

Well, even if she isn't in a coffin, I say, I can't do it alone. This is the job for today and it must be done. I will find another boy to help me if you can't.

By now we are almost to Alice's house. I park in the back pasture, out of sight of the road. I'll bring the pickup around later, I say. For now we don't want anyone knowing that we're here.

Josey worries a hole in the hem of his T-shirt. Is it against the law, what we're doing?

Alice buried her daughter in the backyard so she could visit with her whenever she liked, I say. But now that Alice is moving to Mesa Portales with me, she needs Lorna brought there alongside her. It's the right thing to do and has nothing to do with the law. I think you can understand that.

We walk across the pasture to Alice's house, which looks as if no one has cared for it in a very long time.

Why don't you go check the yard, I say. Make sure Frank Jr. isn't hanging around.

Josey feels no need to ask why we don't want Frank Jr. hanging around, as no one would want that in any circumstance. He just heads off around the back, whistling.

I pick up a broom, give the porch a sweep, and move some potted pink geraniums to the front steps where they can be seen from the road. Inside I open windows so the curtains shift in the breeze, and also I switch on the radio and turn the volume up.

In the bedroom I remove the notes taped to the vanity mirror. *Take one bluepill and one pinkpill. Alice Rose Johnson 67 years old. Do hair. Ask Agatha if you don't know.*

My knees creak as I bend down to get the shovel out from underneath the bureau. I hear Josey open the back door and immediately after that the hollow scrape of the cookie jar lid. Alice loves for Josey to sneak cookies. Frank Jr. is too concerned about his figure, she said once sorrowfully.

In the living room Josey has a cookie in each pocket and one in his mouth. This is a good batch, he says, his mouth full.

Alice will love to hear it, I say. Be sure to tell her.

I myself have a sweet tooth. I believe in cookies and I buy chocolate ones at the store in the biggest bags I can find. The truth is that Alice's cookies are not as tasty as the ones from the store, but the other truth is that I don't like to spend money unnecessarily. So I accept any cookies she presses on me and make do with the disappointment of raisins.

Where's Mrs. Alice?

She's out on a walk, I say. It'd be hard on her to watch Lorna dug up.

I grasp the shovel and slide open the porch door. I stare out into the backyard. Most days I enjoy taking tools in my hand. If I could paint with a hammer or a screwdriver or a lathe, I would do that, but what is more important is to use the tool that gets me closest to what I intend. For me that is ruler first, pencil next, paintbrush last, though a tool or machinery is a delight to me in any other circumstance. But today the shovel feels heavy, and there is no joy in lifting it.

Josey sees my shovel and gets one for himself out of the shed. He shows no concerns in the least. I remind myself that what we are about to do is nothing to hesitate over. It is only bones and flesh and hair that melt back into the richness of the general maw. But I find myself reluctant. When I first knew that I would have to move Lorna, it seemed a straightforward item of business. Perhaps I glossed over it somewhat in my head. How else to explain my reluctance now? It's a chore, the same as any other chore. A job to do. A favor to make.

Josey looks at the grave and then at me. He doesn't speak. He just waits for me to be ready. Am I ready? Well, some things in life are hard. Some things are unpleasant. But the despair I imagine if Josey and I are not successful in this endeavor comes down over me like the sudden sealing of a glass dome. I am sweating and short of breath, even though there is plenty of air available in this backyard, all the air a human could ever need.

Agatha? Josey's forehead is smooth, his eyes clear. He exhibits no worry; he is ready to do whatever chore must be done.

I clear my throat and point with the shovel.

You start at the head and I'll start at the feet, I say. We want to keep it clean and neat. We want to put everything but Lorna back the way we found it.

I plunge the shovel into the grass and gingerly turn over a clump of worm-filled dirt. Alice would be delighted at the loam. But I don't like this overwatered and questionable oasis where Lorna lies. Frankly this whole situation is a travesty.

Josey ignores my instructions to begin digging and instead wraps both arms around the cross, a foot planted firmly on either side. He tugs and strains until the cross pops out. He topples over backward into the lilacs.

I drop my shovel and step on the grave in my hurry to help him up. I don't want him looking around. But he has already flipped over onto his belly and is peering into the hollow center of the lilac stand.

It's all dug up back here already, he calls.

Get up right now, Josey! I grab his wrist. Stop clowning around and finish the job.

I'm not clowning, he says, indignant.

And we freeze at the sound of Frank Jr.'s pickup.

7

GRAB LORNA'S CROSS OFF THE ground and settle it—*thunk*—back into place; it lists only slightly to one side. I throw my shovel over the low adobe wall and then hop over it myself like a spring chicken. Josey follows. We lie on our stomachs, heads down, breathing hard. My heart thrashes in my chest. Frank Jr.'s pickup door slams shut and the screen door creaks open.

Ma! Frank Jr.'s voice from inside the house is muffled. Josey raises himself up onto all fours to get a peek, but I yank his elbow and he collapses back down. We hear the back door open.

Ma! Frank Jr. strides around, opening the shed door, the side gate, examining the trash pile, searching behind and inside everything. If he gets close enough to take a good look at Lorna's grave, he will spot the uprooted shovelful of grass and dirt. But we hear his footsteps move farther away from us along the adobe wall and then they stop, as if he is surveying the land beyond it.

Josey and I stare into each other's eyes. Josey clutches his shovel, and I nod at him to remain calm. We press ourselves down into the dirt and hold our breath until we hear Frank Jr.'s footsteps start up again, then recede, and finally the creak of the metal rocker on the back porch as he sits down. I breathe easier. There will be no upset and fury, no shouting, no further investigation of the yard.

But Frank Jr. is not finished tormenting us, because he begins to sing! It is no mournful tune, no song of loss or sadness, as might befit a son contemplating the poor health of his mother or the grave of his sister. Instead his song is jaunty, it rhymes, and we are trapped. There is nowhere to go, we can only listen.

I am moved by very fine or very poor singing, as both are genuine; I am partial to one and understanding of the other. But Frank Jr. is only mediocre and tries too hard, and so there is nothing in it for anyone, particularly me.

Josey stealthily takes a broken cookie out of his pocket, chews quietly with his mouth closed. His eyes widen as Frank Jr.'s voice grows bolder, more vigorous.

Frank Jr. finishes his song with a flourish, and after that there is silence. We can only wait quietly. The sun is strong. It is best to sleep rather than suffer in it. Josey nods off first, his mouth open, crumbs at the corner of his lips, his hand twitching as if trying to move things in his dream.

I am nearly an old woman, and I doze a bit too.

The sound of Frank Jr.'s pickup wakes me. Josey sleeps on. I lift my head and watch until the dust on the road has settled, and then I gently shake Josey's shoulder.

IT'S TERRIBLE, THE DIGGING UP.

Here we are, Josey and me, our shovels piling up dirt around the grave. I am not one to shirk things, nor am I easily induced into nightmares. In Saskatchewan there were blackened frostbit fingers and toes that fell off. On occasion bodies were kept in the barn until the spring thaw. Beloved horses were shot in the head when foundering. Once my sister and I found a tramp dead in our pasture, his lips and eyelids nibbled off by field mice. But experience in such matters is no help, because death is a horror to living people, and it is in our very bones to feel so. I am subject to this no matter how I try otherwise.

After a long time digging, Josey's shovel hits the coffin lid. He hoots happily because there won't be bones and hair and rotting clothing for us to behold, and also because he has found the treasure first. He digs faster and faster, and it makes me dizzy to watch.

Hold on, I say. We need to conserve our strength.

We lean on our shovels.

Was Lorna a big or little girl? Josey asks.

I never met her so I can't say, I tell him.

Josey goes inside and comes back with a framed photograph of Alice and Lorna. Lorna has her arms wrapped tight around Alice but is smiling at the person taking the photograph. Alice isn't paying attention to the camera at all. Instead she is gazing at Lorna with her whole being.

Lorna isn't big, Josey says, pointing at the photograph. So it shouldn't be too hard.

Too hard for what?

To put her in your pickup.

We're strong, Josey. It won't matter in the least how big she is. Think of all the work we've done at Mesa Portales. Anyway, I'll back the pickup up to the grave, we won't have to carry her far.

We take up our shovels. I tell Josey to dig around the coffin's edges and keep an eye out for the straps used to lower it into the ground, on the theory that we can use them to pull the coffin back up. But any straps are nowhere in evidence, perhaps rotted away or never used at all.

I go inside to find an acceptable substitute, and I take the photograph with me, because I don't care for Lorna's eyes staring at me from it. I put it back on the shelf above the kitchen sink. Sometimes when Alice is washing up, she kisses the tip of her finger and presses it lightly to the photograph.

I rifle through the junk cabinet filled with household odds and ends, scraps of things with uncertain purpose. Alice and I have that in common, never wasting or throwing out things that may be needed, because we are of an era; there's a reason neither of us takes sugar in our coffee. But I can't find anything of use, and I head for the bedroom next.

Alice's scent comes to me when I open the door, as if she has stopped in briefly when I was unawares. I have a good nose and I recognize all the notes: lily of the valley perfume, face powder, plus the unmistakable whiff of old lady. I open the closet door and there are her clothes, carefully hung and with space between each hanger. So the clothes can breathe, Alice says. She loves her clothes, but the truth is her clothes are terrible. Cheap material, gaudy flowered dresses and jersey pantsuits in solid blues of various shades. The color of Lorna's eyes, she says. Poor Frank Jr., whose eyes are only a dull brown and can never compete with the glories of the dead.

I sort through Alice's belts—one white, one black, one navy—but they aren't long enough. On the other side of the closet are her dead husband's clothes, and there's a heavier scent, of dirty saddle. Alice claims he was at one time slim and strong, but when I met him he had a gut on him that wouldn't quit. Well, I have a gut of my own and I don't judge him for that. The point is that his belts will be long. There are two, one black embossed and one plain brown leather, both well worn near the holes where he fastened them. They hang almost to the floor and I take them both.

The sun is now past its zenith. The smell of the raw earth in piles around the grave is rich. Here is the hole in the ground, here is the coffin. Here is Lorna.

We peer down at the coffin, seated more shallowly than seems proper or restful, but this is fortunate for us, and Josey has dug out a few inches all around it.

Let's get these belts underneath the coffin, I say. We'll lift it out, and I'll bring the pickup around. Then we'll go directly to Mesa Portales.

Josey agrees to most things without a word, and when he asks a question it is usually practical, not philosophical. All right, he says, but is there anything to eat first?

All this is a risky business, as someone may come upon us at any moment. But Josey is a growing boy, and so I go back into the kitchen and make a fry-up of eggs, beans, and green chile. Josey gets Alice's amber-colored drinking glasses with the painted strawberries and fills them to the top with lemonade for him and iced tea for me. We slide large bites onto white toast. Afterward Josey makes a peanut butter sandwich with a side of cookies for both of us.

When will you bring Mrs. Alice up there?

As soon as we get Lorna settled.

Mrs. Alice will miss her yard, he says.

That's true, I say. But the soil up there is no good for flowers, and anyway we couldn't waste the water on them.

Where will she sit? Josey asks.

Wherever she wants, I say.

There's only one chair.

That's enough, Josey.

THE EASY PART IS OVER. We have trouble maneuvering the straps underneath the coffin and so we dig the grave out wider. I give Josey a pair of garden gloves because he doesn't want his bare skin to touch the coffin. He hangs down over the edge while I hold his ankles. Don't let go, don't let go! he shouts, and his eyes are wild. But I never would let go of Josey.

He works the middle of the first belt underneath the head of the coffin, then moves on to the foot of the coffin for the next belt. After that I haul him back up.

His teeth are chattering. I don't feel good, he says. He goes inside to lie down on Lorna's old bed.

I pull the pickup around to the backyard, but after I turn off the engine I am unable to move. In fact I am struggling for a deep breath. I have no paper bag, so I open the glove box and stick my face right in it. My breath steadies, but I stay slumped over until Josey taps on the window.

What are you doing, Agatha?

Resting, Josey.

I get out of the pickup. We look at each other.

We are about to yank Lorna up out of her eternal sleep. If I believed in hell I would have concerns. If Alice had whiskey I would give Josey a shot and myself two to calm our nerves. We're all right, Josey, I say, and put a hand on his shoulder.

I let the tailgate down with a bang, and we turn toward the grave.

Now is the hardest part. We stand on opposite sides of the grave and take a belt end in each hand. We are not hopeless in mechanical matters, but we have not been thinking clearly: the belts are not long enough for us to brace ourselves and pull properly. Also my knees don't tolerate it, they creak and buckle.

I let the belts go. We may have to take her out of the coffin, I say.

Josey steps back from the grave. I'm sorry but I won't.

I'm sorry but we will, I say. You're already in this with me. We have to finish this job now before anyone comes along. The reasonable thing is not to dwell on it.

We sit in silence. I consider his unhappiness; but also I need him.

Then Josey volunteers to steal some rope from the neighbor's shed to give us better purchase in pulling the coffin up and out. Right away I understand that's our best chance. He runs off toward the neighbor's place while I keep an eye on the road.

When Josey comes back with a coil of rope we see that Alice's cat is now in the grave, curled up on the coffin.

A cat should know better, I say.

Josey bends down and chirrups. The cat claws its way out of the grave and into his arms. He rubs his cheek against its fur and puts the cat in the pickup cab. We watch it settle itself on the seat.

A mountain lion may get it at Mesa Portales, I say.

I never saw a mountain lion up there, he says, and collects every can of tuna from the kitchen cupboard.

WE DON'T GET IT RIGHT the first time. I hang Josey down by his ankles again while he works two long lengths of rope alongside the belts, twisting each rope with the belt to keep it in place. I pull him up again, and we tie knots in each rope for our hands to lodge against, but Josey's knots slip and so I tie new knots, good ones, because I know all the knots, I can do any knot whatsoever. But even with our fine-tuning the operation is a herky-jerky nightmare. We start and stop, first one of us weakens and then the other, the rope slips in our hands and the coffin crashes back down. Every time Lorna's body thuds around inside it, we pretend we don't hear anything at all.

Finally we stop and drink lemonade with an extra spoonful of sugar each. After that we try again, and this time the coffin heaves up and out. We frantically shuffle in tandem toward the truck until the coffin is over solid ground. Then we drop the ropes immediately and the coffin smacks down onto the earth. We rub our forearms and stand panting, looking at it.

This coffin was once simple pine, but no longer. It might take me some time to forget the sight of it. It is now some other kind of organic matter entirely, dark and splotched, edges softened by rot and damp. Josey gags as we lift it up into the flatbed and cover it over with a tarp to hide it from people, including ourselves. I close the tailgate.

The yard is an eerie shambles. Lorna's cross lies on the lawn. Some might imagine the Devil had come and wrenched an innocent from everlasting slumber. But I don't believe in that and just past this day there will be goodness and joy. It is important to see beyond what is right in front of us.

We refill the grave and try to put the lawn back together. But we are no gardeners or tidiers of flower beds, no thoughtful pruners. We are upset and hurrying, flummoxed by the chunks of sod that we flung aside while digging. Nothing is easily reconstructed, and in the end we shrug helplessly and turn away from it, slide our shovels in the flatbed alongside Lorna. At the last minute I remember the cross, pick it up and jam it into place, then get in the pickup. I don't look back.

Josey trembles all over and clutches the cat close to him. I have a weakness in my hands, and my eyes are tired and scratchy, full of drifting black motes.

Have we done a bad thing, Agatha?

Not at all. We've been very brave.

8

JOSEY FALLS ASLEEP ON THE drive to Mesa Portales, the cat on his lap. I make sure to have nothing in my head. When a troublesome thought comes up, I dismiss it; what will happen to Alice's flowers is a problem for another day. I have exceptional discipline in this habit, it is in fact my truest gift.

I see my house in the distance, far up on the mesa. The roofline is in harmony with the horizon, and I watch the roof rise and dip, rise and dip, along with the road. On the last winding stretch the house disappears from view, but when I emerge up onto the top of the mesa, there is the house in all its glory, and with the ocean canyon beyond it. Each time I arrive and behold this view I am neither happy nor sad, I am nothing, and that is the most perfect state of all. It is in fact a kind of joy, a grateful dissolution.

I pull up next to the grave I dug for Lorna last week. I open the pickup door gently so as not to wake Josey. He is a young person, after all, and I don't mean to make him carry everything. The cat slips out after me, stands briefly with hair on end before darting off behind the house.

I quietly open the tailgate and grab the coffin through the tarp, ease it from the flatbed until one end rests on the ground, the other end on the tailgate. This time the thump and shudder of bones doesn't take me by surprise. I shift the elevated end of the coffin to the ground, push and tug it into position next to the grave.

The passenger-side door swings open. Josey stares at the coffin.

It's all right, Josey, I say. You've helped enough.

I put my hands on the coffin and push.

It crashes down into the grave and lands crookedly, one end of it caught on the rough edge of the grave wall, just a few inches from the bottom. To my relief it doesn't burst open, though it rests at a tilt, a pocket of empty space below one end. In any other circumstance I could not tolerate such a misalignment. But this is new territory entirely.

Josey reaches for his shovel, but I stop him. I'll fill it in later, I say. Let's go inside and wash up. Then supper.

He follows me in. I point at the water bowl. He does a slapdash job, and though I have never bothered about dirt before, today I find that I want him clean. I pour nearly all my stored water into a metal tub and tell him to do the job right.

I'll be outside, I say, and close the door behind me.

The sun is still bright, yet I feel in a dimly lit place. I cover the grave with a tarp and secure the corners with rocks, scatter a thin layer of earth across the top.

The house door swings open and Josey steps outside, tugging on the metal tub. His hair is damp from washing, and his hands are covered in blisters. Leave it, I say. I pull the tub away from the house and dump it out over a patch of Russian thistle.

Josey glances at the grave, then goes back inside without a word. He sits down in my chair and I allow it. I tell him to hold out his hands and I put ointment on his blisters. We don't talk about what we've done.

After supper we go out to the ledge. I sit on the stool I keep out here because it's a chore for me to get up and down off the ground. Josey stretches out next to me. When the cat comes around he picks goatheads out of its matted fur and strokes gently under its chin to hypnotize it. Later he throws a rock into the ocean canyon, and as is our habit we listen into the emptiness until we hear it hit and scuttle below. It makes me think of Alice, how things rattle around inside her and land with scarcely an echo, and I wonder if anything can still sound in her now, anything at all.

Josey throws another rock. Will Mrs. Alice come tomorrow? he asks.

Tomorrow or the next day, I say. What's all this about new shoes?

For school, he says. This year I have to live in La Jara with my uncle during the week. They say I can only come here on Saturdays, maybe. They say going to school is the law.

I open my mouth to tell Josey that what's important is his own law, what is Josey's law. But something stops me. I think of his mother, who right now might be walking to the edge of her property and scouting down the road for my pickup's headlights.

But then I dismiss thoughts of her, because Josey and I are tired, our day has been long, also unusual, and we have only each other to share what has happened in it. Anyway, why dwell on things done or not done? That is called wasted time.

I remember the blackberry buckle and retrieve it from the pickup. Josey gets the fork and the spoon from the house.

We should save some for Mrs. Alice, he says.

All right, I say, and we make sure to leave the largest portion for her.

9

I N THE MORNING I TAKE Josey home. On the way we hatch a plan to sabotage Frank Jr.'s pickup so that he can't come up to bother me anytime soon. Just until Alice gets settled in, I say. After that Frank Jr. will understand that what's done is done.

We don't talk about why Frank Jr. might come to Mesa Portales to bother me. Every day there are more reasons for it, though Josey imagines only Lorna's disheveled grave. Instead we focus on the practical aspects of our problem. Josey agrees that water in the gas tank of Frank Jr.'s pickup should do the trick and that there's no reason to wait.

But when we approach Frank Jr.'s place, we spot him asleep in a hammock strung up between two pines. I drive on by. How insincere he is, snoozing the day away when in his waking hours he bothers everyone with false claims that his mother must be found.

Our immediate difficulty is that Frank Jr.'s pickup will be in his direct line of sight should he wake up. It's no good if he catches Josey in the act. We idle down the road and consider our options.

I can do it at night, Josey says. I can do it more than once.

You are growing into quite a person, Josey, I say. Don't get caught, now.

Don't worry about me, Agatha. He is solemn about his responsibilities.

At Josey's house his mother is waiting for us, hands on hips. She marches Josey inside, tells him to wash up, to hurry, and when he tries to protest her voice rises, Not one word, Josey!

She turns to me. Her eyes are a deep seething chestnut.

I thought we agreed you'd have him home last night, Agatha.

I consider a tone of regret but in the end don't muster it. I had some trouble with the pickup, I say. But what do you know, it started right up again this morning.

She takes this poorly and lets the screen door bang shut behind her.

THE PRESBYTERIAN CEMETERY IS ON a low hill at the edge of town. The cemetery is small, as Presbyterians are scarce around here, and there is a metal fence with a gate to keep the Catholics out. The grave of Alice's husband is a dull scar of poor soil alongside other plots tended with crabgrass or wildflowers, and this satisfies me as a job well done. There are reasons nothing will grow on his grave, no matter how Alice tends and fusses. Those reasons are rock salt and rubbing alcohol, and I keep them handy.

On other occasions I've enjoyed my visits here, but today I find a newly dug hole next to Alice's dead husband. It is three feet by six and five deep, and it is a great distraction to me. I sit back on my heels and admire the fine work of this hole, its even angles and level floor, its perfectly square edges. It is dark and cool, and its earthy smell beckons.

People change in every instant. This is pure science, after all. Only the dead have no age, never move forward in time, and never change again. They die as they are, and that is that, forever. This fact is much lamented by the living—and yet what hypocrisy! For when the dead person was alive the living took any change, such as growing old, as an affront. Alice would not be in the fix she is in if not for this shoddy thinking by the living.

And now here is the chicken-lawyer coming up the hill. He walks right up to Alice's dead husband's salted grave and opens his mouth to speak.

How're your chickens? I say before he can get a word in first.

He's surprised by my question. Apparently he doesn't know he's the chicken-lawyer.

Not laying a lot these days, to tell the truth, he says. I expect it's the heat. What're you doing here, Agatha?

Paying my respects.

He raises his eyebrows at my supplies, then points to a grave festooned in bindweed and plastic roses. That's my mother, right there.

I'm not one to pretend interest in a dead relation. I redirect his attention to the hole next to Alice's dead husband. I hadn't heard of anyone in town passing, I say.

Frank Jr. dug that for Lorna, the chicken-lawyer says.

I make a show of screwing the lid back on the alcohol bottle to cover my alarm at the revelation that Frank Jr. has the talent to dig such a fine grave. Also I understand that this grave will cause me trouble.

Why not leave Lorna to rest in peace where she is? I say.

It'd be difficult to sell the house with Lorna buried in the backyard, he says. Though I've advised Frank Jr. to hold off on moving Lorna until he gets his mother up to Taos, so as not to upset her.

It's a disgrace that he wants to sell her house out from under her in order to benefit himself, I say.

He shrugs. Most folks would argue that Mrs. Johnson will also benefit, once she gets adjusted to her new home. In any case Frank Jr. is a man in his prime and he wants to strike a new path for himself.

He is a fool on an errand, I say.

I thought you might have some sympathy for him, the chicken-lawyer says, being an artist type yourself. Frank Jr. wants his own chance.

Have you heard him sing?

He hesitates. I haven't had the pleasure.

I examine him with interest, as he does not seem quite truthful.

The fact is I saw your pickup headed this direction, he says, and I came to have a talk. I wonder when you last saw Mrs. Johnson.

First the new grave and now this! I make sure to give a scant answer, so none of my words come back to haunt me.

Why? I say.

The chicken-lawyer looks at me appraisingly. Frank Jr. hasn't seen his mother in two days and has concerns. He is making up a search party. Seeing as how you are such a friend to Mrs. Johnson, I assume you would be willing to help in this endeavor.

He says this last part like setting a trap. But I am not such a fool as to put my foot in it.

Why would I waste time searching for someone who doesn't

need to be found, I say. You are on a wild-goose chase. I saw Alice this very morning in her own kitchen. She had a lunch packed and a full canteen. She likes to walk to her family's old place near the reservoir.

That's quite a distance for her, he says.

She does it most every day without difficulty, I say. She is a grown woman who enjoys a walk and it is not a crime. I drove by Frank Jr.'s place not thirty minutes ago and saw him napping in broad daylight. He wasn't concerned about his mother or organizing anything in the least.

Likely he's tired from being up all night worrying, the chicken-lawyer says.

Frank Jr. might want to get out of bed earlier if he cares to see his mother, I say.

I gather my supplies and head toward my pickup. It's fortifying to have the last word, I always enjoy it.

But the chicken-lawyer spoils my satisfaction by calling after me. Frank Jr. suspects you are hiding her up at Mesa Portales! And I know for a fact Mrs. Johnson didn't sleep in her own bed last night, he adds, because Frank Jr. and I went and had a look.

I stop walking.

Now, Agatha, don't get upset. He holds his palms up as if to ward off an attack. Let's say that you are and that she is. In fact it'd be understandable if she were staying with you for a night or two before she goes to her new place. Saying her good-byes and whatnot. Better just to say so and save us all the worry.

I don't answer because I am thinking carefully.

Perhaps you might consider the place in Taos for yourself as well, he says. It seems a good solution, as you and Mrs. Johnson could continue to enjoy your friendship.

I'm not leaving Mesa Portales, I say.

He sighs. I got a call from New York.

I smile.

Turns out your lawyer doesn't understand how things work around here. He gestures at the freshly sprinkled and salted grave. I wonder if you heard about Alice's husband. The way he passed.

You mean his heart?

Is that what Alice told you?

I frown.

He turned up dead in an arroyo because he messed around with the wrong young girl, the chicken-lawyer says. The official report states that it was a hunting accident, but this girl had older brothers and a daddy. I am telling you this in confidence, though most everyone around here knows and approves.

It's no shock that Alice's husband was even more terrible than I knew or that people enact their own justice. But the wind is knocked out of me because Alice has not told me this secret. Also I don't care to learn things by surprise, as in my experience there is rarely such a thing as a good one.

My point is that things around here might operate a little different than what you might be used to, he says.

I laugh to show him that I am not rattled by his warning. However Alice's husband met his demise is of no concern to me, I say.

He puts a hand on his heart. Agatha, you do remind me of my sister.

If he imagines he can pull a topic out of thin air and interest me in it, he is wrong. But still he yammers on!

Listen to me, Agatha. My own sister moved away to Denver while I was in law school. Folks said she had come into her own and that it suited nobody but her. I think you might have some understanding of what I mean. I am not unsympathetic to you. But this is a serious business.

I regard him closely. He does not lose his nerve when I do this, as has happened to other people on similar occasions, and it seems to me that a kind of offer has been extended and he is waiting for my answer. The fact is that the chicken-lawyer walks like a man and talks like a man, but also he has told me that his sister is a person I would recognize, and he has said it without judgment. It is so difficult to trust. But I am in a situation full of holes, and perhaps he can help me avoid falling in one.

Let's suppose Alice is staying up at Mesa Portales with me, I say.

Is she or isn't she?

She might be.

Well, for how long?

A few days, I say. Just until she gets her mind around things.

The chicken-lawyer puts his eyebrows together in a show of deliberation. I'll advise Frank Jr. to give his mother a few days' grace. But I'll be making sure all promises are kept and all things are accounted for.

Those are things I believe in also, I say.

We squint at each other, then shake on it.

I might ask why you yourself are here in this town, I say. Doesn't seem like enough lawyer business to keep you.

I worked a few years in Albuquerque after law school, he says. I was there when Lorna died and I helped her family through it. But the city didn't suit me. There is nowhere more beautiful in this world than right here.

I am discomfited that the chicken-lawyer and I share some affinities.

Well, Agatha, he says, you consider what I've said. Big-city stuff won't fly around here. You're better off going on back to where you came from. That is the general opinion. I am simply passing it along.

Then he clears his throat and spits his chaw on the ground. He is once again the chicken-lawyer that I have known previously, the one with dirty feet up on his desk. He may yet be wearing a sly costume, and I remind myself to be cautious.

He heads down the hill, whistling.

10

ONCE THE CHICKEN-LAWYER IS GONE I look again at the empty grave. It will be quite a scene when Frank Jr. tries to dig Lorna up from Alice's backyard. There will be piles of dirt and many curses thrown. He may dig all the way to China, but still he won't find her. Though all that is acceptable as long as I am not suspected.

I drive to Alice's place. In her bedroom I get the suitcase from her closet and open it on the bed. This suitcase is cornflower blue with a silver clasp, and inside is a handful of lavender sprigs tied with twine. I leave the lavender and add Alice's sky-blue pantsuit, the white shirt with a round collar, slippers, and a nightgown. Also hairpins, panties, and the hand mirror with a hummingbird stitched in bright thread on velvet backing. I take Lorna's brooch from the clock, wrap it in a handkerchief, and tuck it inside one of the slippers.

On the hook behind the door is the denim shirt Alice wears for gardening. Along its collar are three black-edged holes. Alice claimed that one day the sun turned so sharp and angry that it fried those holes right through the fabric. More likely it was your husband got careless with his cigarette, I said. She said, Why must you be that way, Agatha?

The last time this shirt touched Alice's skin, she was tired and ready for bed. I'd tried to help her off with it. She watched my fingers tussle with the buttons, she chuckled and brushed my hands away. She undid the buttons herself, slowly, until it hung open to show the faded cream of her brassiere. She unhooked my overalls and helped me tug the shirt from my broad shoulders, then smiled and lay down on the bed. I eased in next to her like so many times before. The breeze came in through the window and across our bellies, and she took my hand and sighed with pleasure. We stared up at the web of ceiling cracks as if at clouds on a summer afternoon. I hadn't felt a comfort like it in quite some time.

I fold the denim shirt and make sure the edges are straight and square. I add it to the suitcase and buckle the latches. I put the suitcase in the pickup and refill my water jugs at the backyard hose. The purple stock and white daisies are wilting in the heat, and even the pink hollyhocks are not so proud as usual. I take the hose and go from plant to plant, making my way around the yard. The leaves on the lilac bushes are now wilted and edged with brown, and I make sure to keep my eyes firmly on the upper branches and not on the ground.

Finally there is nothing left to water but Lorna's grave. Alice prides herself on keeping it lush and well tended. I think of what Josey and I have done to it. I don't want to see the grave now, its ruin, though I know a good watering will help the grass recover. But when I reluctantly turn to it, I see an unexpected sight.

I am a person with very sharp eyes, and I am standing just three feet from where Lorna used to lie. Yet there is no evidence that Josey and I ever set shovel to this grave. The grass covering it is smooth and I see no seam around the edges, no raggedy outline or shovel marks, no churned-up quality of earth. Not even the space below, the space that Lorna in her coffin used to fill, is evident; there is no sinkage, no flattening of the grass mound, no sideways listing of the wooden cross.

In fact I have never seen the grave so tidy. It is as if it never happened, as if Lorna had never been disturbed at all.

11

O N THE DRIVE BACK TO Mesa Portales I concentrate on what there is to see. I watch flat-bottomed clouds scudding rapidly across the sky. The scarcity of trees, I prefer that. There is no bloating, no false inflation of value simply by virtue of more greenery. Where there is a tree, it can be properly admired.

But the vision of Lorna's pristine grave, its ominous sameness, has blotted out any pleasure I might take in the glory of a cottonwood or pine. My back and knees are sore from digging, clear evidence of what Josey and I have done; but on occasion I have been mistaken and not seen the world as it is. For this reason it is urgently in my mind to check below the tarp covering the grave at Mesa Portales.

Yet when I arrive at my house, there is Veronica. Today, of all days! She sits on the ledge with her back to me. She must hear the pickup but doesn't turn her head, which makes me cross. Why should I go to her? She is the one who has shown up uninvited. I park and head toward the house without acknowledging her. The cloth covering the canvas on the easel is slightly askew, and so I know that she has already been inside.

I look out the window at the grave. The tarp scattered over with dirt is excellent camouflage, but next to that is the large pile of earth yet to be shoveled back in. The overall effect will require explanation, because Veronica is a person who is alive and noticing in every way. I don't mean breathing, eating, walking, talking. Anyone is capable of those things. I mean that she is open and receptive, that she has her antennae out for life. She was undeveloped when I met her, but I saw that she had the essential quality. All she lacked was guidance.

Early on Veronica told me, I had parents, but they didn't believe in education, only religion, and they think art history is a devilish invention. I've left them behind, I've done everything on my own. Her eyes were dark and burning when she said this.

I patted her hand, because of course I understood. A person can spring from their own head and make their own way. That is my life, after all.

She has not come to Mesa Portales in some time. It's been months—eight, in fact—since she spoke with me about her problem. Yet after all my sound advice to her on that occasion, I have not heard a word since.

The first time Veronica appeared, I put paintings one by one on the easel and indicated that she and the young man with her should stand as far away as possible. They flattened themselves against the back wall. I observed them as they looked. The young man lasted less than a minute before he began spouting nonsense. He didn't know how to see or how to be silent, and so would never recognize the important things. I told him to shut up, and he did.

Veronica said nothing, only relaxed her face and eyes. She was someone who tried to see. The young man's inanities had not distracted her, likely because she was used to them. I suppose he was her boyfriend. But they were no match. Everything about Veronica was superior.

She instinctively knew to let my painting reveal itself. It was clear to me when this happened: when the lines began to shift and move, when they altered her way of feeling. She gave a silent start, enough to make the young man frown. She kept looking, moved a step forward, a step back, and I knew that it was working on her.

The young man, however, was impatient. When he began photographing my things—the metal trough where I store cooking items, the shelf where I keep my shirts—I ordered him outside. It is time for you to go, I said to him. Do not come back.

I'm not a small woman and he wasn't a large young man. When I walked toward him, he backed toward the door. Come on, Vero, let's go. When she didn't break her gaze, he broke it for her, grabbing her by the arm. She turned away from the painting but not toward him. With his dirty paw on her, she looked only at me, and I saw how she moved her hand over her heart without knowing what she did.

The young man glared. Let's go, he said to Veronica.

I want *you* to go, I said. She can stay.

They stared at each other, surprised. She pulled her arm away. They went outside and bickered. After a while I heard the car start up and next the crunch of tires on the dirt road. I thought I had been mistaken about her. But the door opened again and Veronica stepped back inside.

She stayed a week, that first time. From the beginning she took pains to be harmonious. She made dinner, she arranged the plate and bowl and fork on the table correctly, and she knew better than to bother me when I was working. I said things and she wrote them down, and it turned out to be true that this was fortifying to me.

Veronica has a talent for attention and she is purposeful, a quality not appreciated by everyone. The professors and fellow students in her graduate program think her overambitious and irritating; they say that she does not relax, that she tells no jokes. They make bets over when she will fail or drop out or fall in love. There is an expectation that I will sleep with them, she said, but I will not.

What about that fool you arrived with, I'd asked. Were you sleeping with him?

He had a car, she said. I couldn't have come here otherwise.

We never discussed why she came in the first place, because of course she had come for me. Many did at that time, though it's true that no one has appeared in the last year or two. This world is a fickle place, and I have not been out and about in it as much.

Every night Veronica made herself a bed on the floor. She always slept immediately and with abandon, her breath easy and her body relaxed. Occasionally she flung out an arm abruptly or held conversations with people I did not know. In the mornings she woke and while still on the floor stretched her limbs to wring her waking self from her dreams—and also she smiled because she knew I was watching.

In fact she was straightforward about our bargain, the terms of which we never discussed yet understood implicitly. I was to be studied and taken notes about, and she was the person to do those things; I could study her in return, enjoy the flame of her beauty and be warmed by it. Well, she had the vanity of youth, and also she was not a small-minded or fearful person. Over time I simply grew fond of her, and always I have appreciated her ability to see.

At the end of that first week, I gave Veronica a ride back to Albuquerque. This has been quite a honeymoon, she said to me, grinning. She rolled down the pickup window for air, and her hair billowed wildly around her face.

Of course there had been no honeymoon, it was not that kind of relation. But I enjoyed this tone and remembered her often. The next time I gave a lecture at the university, I asked Dan to find her for me.

Do you know her? I asked.

Everyone knows Veronica, he said. His face was watchful. He did find her, and she kept me company at the reception afterward. I saw that I had not been mistaken about her, and later, when I sent her money for a car, she made no false protest. She understood that I was right to give her the money for the car, that it was important to me that she see my work, and also that she had nothing to fear from me. After that she came to Mesa Portales regularly.

She has a ruthlessness about her that I admire, a ruthlessness for the things she cares about. She cares about me, and I would never mind how ruthless she was on my behalf. She is willing to leave some things behind in order to have other things. I approve of this quality, though Alice does not. In fact they don't understand each other, and the uneasiness between them suits me, because I like firm lines and sharp divisions.

Not long after I met Veronica, Alice arranged a picnic at the creek near her back pasture. She spread a large star-patterned quilt on the ground and Veronica relaxed onto it in an easy posture, ready for conversation. But Alice ignored her and instead flung open the lid of a wicker sewing basket repurposed for our picnic. She put her hand within its pink silk lining and pulled out a handful of strawberries, arranged them in a neat row on the quilt in front of me, and watched as I ate them one by one. Only then did she offer Veronica a dull sandwich from a brown sack, asked polite questions about her university coursework, and later sent her on her way.

I'm not in the house long before Veronica opens the door. She smiles uncertainly, her eyes flicking from the ground to my face, back and forth, as if unsure of her welcome. She is twenty-five now; I thought of her on her birthday last month. The angles of her face are sharper and her shoulders have become more sinewy, less rounded. She has a sprinkle of freckles across her nose and good color on her arms and legs. Also I can smell the happiness on her. We haven't seen each other in eight months, and she is happy.

I busy myself with dishes in the washing tub. Along with the happiness she smells faintly of lavender. I know she's looking at the covered canvas and wondering why there are no new paintings stacked deep along the wall. Later she will jot down what we have talked about, any new work I might yet show her, any words I have said.

On occasion I have run into her in town, where there is no need for her to be, talking to people with her notebook in her hand. Once I caught her sharing a cigarette with the postmistress, and I went right up and demanded a package I claimed to be expecting, a package the postmistress had no doubt overlooked in her desire to smoke rather than do the work the government pays her for. The postmistress only laughed, stubbed out her cigarette, and went to check for my package.

I sent Veronica on her way, and when the postmistress came back she had no package but did have coffee cake, and we sat together in her garden and discussed the row of sunflowers she'd planted along the wall, which in bloom produced a harmony that I admired.

I have water jugs in my pickup, I say to Veronica now.

She makes three trips back and forth to bring them in. She doesn't ask why I don't move the pickup closer to the house to make it easier to unload them. She knows that if the pickup is not parked in its proper place it will interfere with the view, and also that if she wants to be at Mesa Portales, if she wants more notes to scribble down in her little notebook, she has to do what I say. Over time this has been agreed to between us without any words at all. Over time it seemed to me that her notebook ceased to be the reason she came.

When she finishes I sit in the chair because I am the one with old knees. Veronica sits easily on the floor, cross-legged like a child. She gestures casually out the window toward the grave. What're you doing over there? she asks.

An herb garden, I say. Or possibly I'll put a tree there.

You don't like trees.

Sometimes I do.

Next she gestures pointedly at the easel, the covered canvas. Here is her true line of inquiry. No doubt she wonders if it is the same blank canvas, after all her time away. She turns to me with this silent question, waits to hear. But there's no new painting and I can't say when there will be. For some time now there has not been another one, and perhaps it is not important that there should ever be another one again. Anyway, today is a day for a different business. I feel the tired dullness in my head, the feeling that rises up when things are not in order.

Aren't you even glad to see me, Agatha?

Well, the truth is I am glad to see her. Veronica is a breath of fresh air, a balm, a reminder to me that there may still be pleasure in this world. She can help me keep my worries at bay until I go back to Alice's place, where everything that remains to be done must be done by me, because I am the one to do things. But also I'm offended that Veronica has stayed away so long.

I have some news, she says. I defended my dissertation a couple of weeks ago. I brought a copy for you.

She takes a manuscript out of her bag.

Read me the title page, I say.

She clears her throat. *Joy and Innocence in the Work of Agatha Smithson: An Examination of Works on Canvas, 1968–1973.*

I smile in spite of myself. Over time Veronica's course of study has narrowed to a particular era of painting: my era. Or, as she likes to call it, the Era of Agatha. This pleases me, though also it feels mildly fatuous. But Veronica believes that such broad announcements play well and argues, Don't you have a bounty of work to back it up? Well, I take her point and don't disagree.

She offers the manuscript. It's for you.

Leave it over there. I point to the wall near the canvas.

She obediently—good girl—puts the manuscript down where I've told her to. It is so like an altar offering that I can't help but laugh and she does too, because she is a quick study.

What's that? she asks, stretching out her hand as if she might touch the beadwork on the purse around my middle. But I wave her hand away.

Where's your car? I ask.

It needs new brakes, she says. I took the bus. Uncle Felix gave me a lift from town.

Well, get new brakes.

I can't afford them. I'm not a graduate student anymore, she says. No more stipend. I need a position.

You've known this time was coming, I say. Why haven't you planned for it?

There is a silence in which both of us consider the eight months since I've last seen her. She looks away.

How about lunch? I say.

Over time Veronica has developed a tolerance for my peanut butter and tomato sandwiches. As we eat she tells me about her dissertation defense, how she was keyed up and nervous, how the three professors, all men, began by challenging her, but as the discussion went on the tone changed to one of intense and equal conversation; she described this change with jubilation.

I was able to talk to them about your work, she says, in a way that they hadn't engaged with it before. When they realized that I know you personally, they wanted to hear more. I did well. I hope I made you proud.

You have no obligation to make me proud, I say.

Maybe not, but I wanted to honor you. We talked in particular about the series from two years ago. They're such wonderful paintings.

Yes, I say.

Well, *wonderful* isn't exactly the right word, she says. It's not expansive enough.

I nod.

Of course the reproductions included in the dissertation are only mimeographs, she says, but I brought your monograph to show them.

Any reproduction whatsoever is a useless thing, I say. My monograph was printed at a superior level by a fine Belgian press, and yet the reproductions fail in every way. I will never do another one.

But you must do another one, she says. For your legacy.

What Veronica says is not unreasonable. There are certain things that must be done if one wishes to be remembered. In the past I have cared about those things, but today my mind is turning over other commitments, other legacies, pitfalls still to see my way around. So I ignore what Veronica has said and I eat my sandwich in silence.

But Veronica has more thoughts to air.

People are interested in you, she says, specifically in where you came from and how you came to be an artist. Your childhood influences, that kind of thing.

Even the dissertation panel, she adds, they weren't knowledgeable about your worldview. They wanted to hear as much as I could tell them. Which wasn't much, really.

Do you want to know what I told them? she says.

You could at least say *something*, Agatha.

She says, They asked about your position on feminism.

I stand up, irritated, because I am not a feminist. I am Agatha.

I put my plate in the washing pail and glance over at the dissertation. *Submitted by Vero Miller.*

I frown. Why are you still going by Vero?

This is not a new argument between us. When she first appeared at Mesa Portales, she introduced herself as Vero. Short for Veronica, she'd said, and wrinkled up her nose. Vero is an affectation, I told her at the time. I've only ever called her Veronica.

But she doesn't react, which is unlike her.

I'm going outside, I say abruptly.

Veronica follows me to the ledge, where the view is magnificent at any time and in any light. Yet she persists in talking instead of seeing. She has changed the way we go about our business; she has thinned the line between us. My heart beats, too fast. I sit down on my stool.

I know you probably won't read it, she says. The dissertation. But I wanted to bring it to you anyway, to thank you.

So you're wrapping things up. I say this lightly, also sarcastically.

No, no. She sits down on the ground and looks up at me from below. I wanted to talk to you, Agatha.

I stare across the ocean canyon and wait for more. She has never been hard to lead through silence. It is a weakness in her, this need to please. But today I feel a resistance, a solidity inside her that is new. She is different in some way that I can't put my finger on.

I want to write a book, she says abruptly. A book about you. A biography.

No, I say. I wouldn't like that at all.

If you wait until you're dead, you'll have no say in the matter. This book could be a collaboration between us.

You mean it'd be a feather in your cap.

She sighs. Just think about it, Agatha. It's going to happen one way or another. Who would you trust more than me to write it?

I examine her face for signs of guile. Also I admire the arch of her eyebrows and the shine in her eyes, the pale blue ribboning of veins near her temples where she has tucked her hair behind her ears.

She mistakes my inspection of her for interest in her idea, and she leans forward to press her point. Anyone could go back and interview the other artists at the Slip, she says, and write about how you got your start. But I know you from *here*, from Mesa Portales, where you have done your most important work. And I care about you, Agatha. I'm not just anybody.

A storm has formed on the horizon, a cluster of dark clouds; the vertical gestures within them signify rain. I see the eagerness on Veronica's face. But I stay silent, I wait, and soon all the hope drains from her.

We watch the far-off spikes of lightning.

Is it really that hard, she asks, to trust me?

How a person is expected to answer such a question is difficult to figure. But a suspicion stirs inside me.

And you, I say, have you tidied up after yourself since we last talked?

It's a great concession that I bring this subject up first. But I want to put her on the back foot.

She flushes. Everything is fine. She hesitates, her mouth open as if to say more, but she doesn't.

All right, I say, relieved. Well done. You're welcome to spend the night. I can drop you off in town tomorrow.

A low rumble of thunder breaks over the ocean canyon, and the cloud shadows shift in our direction. I hear Veronica take a deep breath.

I don't want to lie to you, she says. I had the baby.

This statement is outrageous, in fact so unsettling that I stand up, agitated. Then I make myself sit back down on my stool, as if I haven't been alarmed at all. I settle my hands on my thighs.

That's not what we decided, I say.

But she doesn't wilt and comply as she usually does. Instead she lifts her chin. I don't expect you to approve, she says.

Well, did you give it up for adoption?

No.

Where is it? I look around, because she must have stashed a swaddled bundle somewhere.

Back in Albuquerque, she says, with a touch of impatience. I wouldn't bring a baby out here, not before I told you.

So that's why you came. Not because of your schoolwork.

She cuts her eyes at me over *schoolwork*. I came to give you the dissertation. I hadn't planned to mention the baby.

This is very upsetting, I say.

We thought it would be, she says faintly. We knew you would disapprove.

And are you together now, you and Dan?

No.

And Melinda, what is her opinion of all this?

Veronica frowns. She's not leaving him. You know how she is. Anyway, I don't want that.

She stands up and brushes off her calves, straightens her skirt. I see a flash of waist, paler than the rest of her.

I'm not sorry about the baby, she says. I'm glad. You can't imagine what it's like, Agatha. It's wonderful, I didn't expect it.

I take it all as a kind of violent rudeness, that this was going on and I knew nothing about it, that I found out only because Veronica drove out here to give me her silly term paper. It's ridiculous that anything goes on anywhere other than Mesa Portales, that one can isolate oneself from the world but still it goes about its business.

Well, I say, it's nonsense for you to talk about writing a book. You will not have time, your hands will be full, in fact they already are. I'm sorry to tell you that but it's true.

Her face turns an angry red. Why are you always willing to help Dan but never me?

More nonsense, I say.

You helped him get a faculty appointment when he needed it, she says.

So a biography about me is actually for you, I say.

It's for both of us, she says.

I didn't think we were in this for scratching each other's backs.

Agatha! I care about you.

When I don't answer she stares out over the ocean canyon, but her eyes are unfocused and unseeing. I wait because she'll speak before I do, she can never outlast me.

But to my surprise she stands up and steps away from the ledge. If that's the way it is with us, she says, then I need to go home. Can I take your pickup?

Why the big hurry? I say.

I have to get back to the baby.

Well, did you leave it alone in its bed?

Of course not.

Then it will be well taken care of, whoever is supervising it.

She makes an impatient sound. I'll bring the pickup back tomorrow! I'll ask Dan to follow in his car and take me back to Albuquerque. You'd like that, wouldn't you, to see your favorite child.

He doesn't cross me like you do, I say.

It's Dan's baby too, Agatha! Please, lend me your pickup.

Absolutely not, I say. What if I have an emergency? I'm an old woman.

She laughs, but it's not a pretty sound. She paces back and forth, crosses her arms over her chest. She is under the sway of something other than reason and good sense. I suppose hormones.

You are not the only one with concerns, I say. I have plans of my own. I can't take time out for this little business of yours. I'll drive you into town tomorrow. You can catch the Greyhound from there.

I say these things definitively. But Veronica has a mutinous expression on her face. It's shocking how badly behaved she is when she doesn't get her way. Well, I wash my hands of her.

By now the sun is dropping. I am ready for dark, for the nighttime ocean canyon. Though tonight Veronica has ruined that for me. I need to feel my house around me and consider my own concerns. I take the keys from the pickup's ignition in case Veronica gets any funny ideas. I should have known that she would at some point compromise us with a child.

INSIDE MY HOUSE I CAN'T settle. I go from chair to window and back many times over. Veronica and Dan didn't take my advice, after all my trouble on their behalf. When have babies ever been for the better, if other ambitions are inside a person?

All this fuss makes me think of Julien. He was my first and finest friendship with a young person. He appeared at my studio in New York just a few months before I left it, a young man in a suit looking for something more in his life. By that time I had argued with all my friends and given up on many people, because the quality of person one encountered was so often disappointing. But when Julien appeared he was a surprise and a joy. He came to see my paintings and stayed for days, listening to me, and he instinctively recognized that I had superior knowledge in areas that mattered. That at least is how I prefer to remember him. I have often extolled his virtues to Veronica, so that she can learn. But it's also true that he later disappointed me, and I must take care to never let Veronica do the same.

In the past I have occasionally written to Julien to tell him how well I am doing, but of course there is no address for him and so I throw these letters on the pile for burning. Lately my memories of him have faded, and anyway it is best if I never hear from him again.

Still, I sometimes wish for Julien to see that I am back to myself. I would show him the house and the ocean canyon, the sky, the papery quality of the dust on the hottest days. Also we would have a family dinner. Veronica has been eager for this. How is Julien? she once asked. What news of Julien?

Dan was with us when she asked this, and he put his sandwich down as if he had lost his appetite, because he does not like the idea of Julien.

In the end I told Veronica that Julien has moved far away to Norway, and so it is unlikely that they will ever meet. But even now I like to imagine them all here together, and in my head I move them around like characters in a play, a delightful comedy. Mesa Portales is the greatest stage of all, for so many things. Though if they were all truly here, they might quarrel and compete for my attention.

LATER I STEP OUTSIDE. VERONICA is sleeping in the pickup flatbed, as we did on a drive out to see Shiprock at dawn. On that occasion we stopped for the night near a small creek, where Veronica collected wood and I cooked our supper over a fire, soup that was water with a bit of rabbit and a few beans that never quite softened and some wild greens we found tossed in. For Veronica this was a novel entertainment, but for me it was simply a routine from my youth. Well, those days with her are done.

I walk quietly to the pickup and listen until I am assured of Veronica's slumbering breath. Then I turn toward the grave. My knees crack when I bend down over it. I push aside the rock and lift the tarp's corner.

And what relief! My flashlight beams down on the rotted wood of Lorna's coffin. The world is as I believe it to be.

Though as I walk back toward the house another problem occurs to me, as two things can't exist at the same time: firstly Lorna at Mesa Portales, and secondly an unsullied grave at Alice's house. But I am willing to accept such a mystery, as all in all the result is firmly in my favor.

12

VERONICA HAS STOLEN INSIDE IN the night and is now asleep on the floor. Her linen blazer—professorial, as she aspires to be—is folded neatly under her head for a pillow. I look to understand how she is different, but she is the same: the soft hollow between her collarbones, the callouses on her elbows and heels, the scar on one knee from a spiny locust bush. It is as if there had been no baby at all, ever, inside of her, and she can therefore move forward as we always have.

Veronica, I say. Time to get up.

She rolls over onto her back, covers her face with her arm, groans. Her shirt is damp across her breasts. She is leaking milk. She is a cat without her kittens, a cow without her calf. And so on.

I know she wants coffee. I consider not making it but then I do. By the time I finish, she has tugged her blazer back on. She's tired, her mouth tight. I offer her the coffee.

Thank you, Agatha, she says. Her green eyes are tender as she takes it with one hand and tucks her hair behind her ear with the other. I think the world of her all over again.

I don't ask about the baby. What kind it is, its name. We have awoken with an unspoken agreement to be as we have always been, and the baby is a bomb we don't want to explode on ourselves. We are behaving carefully.

How's Josey? she asks.

He says he's done with school.

She laughs, as if Josey's words were foolish. I hope you straightened him out. He'll listen to you.

He can decide for himself, I say. School is not the whole world.

That gets her attention. You're a university professor! she says. How could you not encourage Josey to go to school?

Are these your newfound motherly instincts kicking in, I say. I myself have no university degree and only as much schooling as Josey has right now. I live out here, no different than him.

It's entirely different!

I was born in Nowhere, Saskatchewan, I say. I milked cows every morning before dawn.

Well, you managed to escape all that, she says. Why can't you help Josey do the same?

Somebody has to milk the cows, I say.

Veronica shakes her head because she doesn't like this answer, but nowhere is it required that I please her with my opinions. The truth is I don't mean what I have said, not for Josey, but also I don't like to change a good thing.

I DRIVE AND VERONICA RIDES shotgun. There is a feeling of old times. But as we approach Alice's place, the sky turns a pitiless iron blue and a heavy dread settles in my chest. This heaviness is not a mystery: it is dread of the thing at Alice's house that still needs doing. My hands tremble on the steering wheel.

Alice has visitors, Veronica says, pointing at Frank Jr.'s pickup and the sheriff's car parked out front.

I feel a further twinge of trouble.

Her son, I say. He and I are coming to an agreement over things.

I press on the gas and put Alice's house behind us.

What things?

Alice is moving up to Mesa Portales with me, I say.

Veronica turns to look at me. Why would she move to Mesa Portales?

Why wouldn't she.

No flowers will grow up there, she says. Also you don't have running water or electricity.

And you think running water and electricity are important things.

Most people think those are important things, she says.

Alice is not most people, I say.

Alice is the best of most people, Veronica says, but she is absolutely most people. I can't believe her son is going along with it.

Her son has not entirely accepted the idea of Mesa Portales yet, I say. He intends to move her to an old folks' home in Taos. But what he wants is not important. What is important is what Alice wants.

Be realistic, Agatha! How will you get any work done if you have to take care of her?

That is the question you should be asking yourself about your own life, I say.

We're not talking about me right now, she says. You won't have a moment's peace if Alice is living with you. Remember that business with the cane when I was here last fall?

There is no business with a cane, I say. It is simply a cane that has been misplaced and she wishes to find it.

But Veronica is shaking her head. My grandmother lived with us when I was young, she says. I know how these things go: old people fixate on things for no reason at all and then drive everyone crazy. They lose things because they are losing themselves. Alice won't get better, only worse. She's not the same anymore.

You are not the same anymore either, I say, and indicate the damp stains on her shirt.

But she dismisses my solid argument. The difference is that I am moving deeper into my life, she says, while Alice is moving out of hers.

What she says is more true than she knows, but still I feel a rush of anger and slam on the brakes. Veronica catches herself on the dash with one hand and holds up the other in mute apology.

Anyway, Alice won't want to leave her own house, she says. Her daughter is buried in the backyard, for God's sake.

Alice's daughter will also be moving up to Mesa Portales, I say.

Veronica is startled. There must be a regulation against that, she says.

If Alice wants to move her daughter's grave, there's no crime in it, I say. Anyway, we're not hampered by regulations out here.

She stares out the window. Your life will be entirely changed, Agatha. It'll be impossible for you to work.

Work is not the only thing in life, I say.

Veronica laughs, incredulously, as if I have made an outlandish joke; but I surprise myself by feeling it to be true. I would do anything possible, anything at all, to keep Alice with me.

I PARK OUT FRONT OF the chicken-lawyer's office. I lean across Veronica and open the passenger-side door so that she has no choice but to slide out immediately. Then I yank the door shut again.

The bus stops there, I say, pointing across the street. You take care now, Veronica.

But before I can pull away, the chicken-lawyer steps out onto his porch and calls to me. Agatha, hold up! He hurries down the steps and peers into the pickup.

Mrs. Johnson's not with you?

Anyone with eyes can see that Alice is not with me, so I don't bother to reply. But his gaze has already shifted away because there is Veronica, waving at him. Her smile is big, like sunshine.

I'm a friend of Agatha's, she says to him. May I use your phone? It's long distance, but I'll pay you for it. She lifts her purse.

Why sure, he says. Come on in and make your call while Agatha and I have a talk.

Veronica doesn't look at me as she heads toward the office.

Beautiful hair, the chicken-lawyer says to her as she passes him.

She awards him a faint smile. I got it from my mother. She bounds up the porch steps.

Well, you thank your mother for me! His face falls when she doesn't answer.

We watch her through the window as she picks up the phone and dials. The chicken-lawyer sighs and turns back to me, now all business.

Frank Jr. roared through here in his truck not an hour ago, stinking drunk, he says. The sheriff followed him out to his mother's place. Frank Jr. was shouting about driving up to Mesa Portales to get her.

The thought of Frank Jr. stepping foot on Mesa Portales fills me with a bracing rage. I take a deep full breath and feel my hands steady.

The chicken-lawyer keeps right on talking. The sheriff and I agree it's best to head off any trouble, he says. Frank Jr. is sleeping it off in his childhood bed, and the sheriff will escort Mrs. Johnson up to the place in Taos in the meantime. I was hoping she was with you, to save the sheriff the drive out to Mesa Portales.

He waits for me to respond, but I am thinking things over.

His face grows reproving at my silence. Why would you think it's a good idea to leave Mrs. Johnson all alone up there while you're gallivanting around town with that one? He jerks his head in Veronica's direction.

But now I am far ahead of him.

I drove Alice to the place in Taos last night, I say. I've come around to your view that she needs more than I can do for her.

The chicken-lawyer looks skeptical, so I point to the suitcase in the back of the pickup. I'm on my way there right now, to bring her a few things until her house gets packed up.

You don't mind if I take a look.

Go right ahead, I say.

He opens the suitcase, nods, satisfied by the folded clothes, and buckles the suitcase back up. Well, it's the best place for her, he says. At least she got out to Mesa Portales one last time before she went. She's always been real fond of the place.

I frown, because how would he know what Alice was fond of?

Veronica opens the screen door and shuffles glumly down the porch steps.

The chicken-lawyer reaches out to touch her arm. Everything fine? he asks.

She sidesteps him and crosses the street to the bus stop, sits down on the curb with her shoulders slumped.

Pretty girl, the chicken-lawyer says. Lacks a cheerful spirit, though.

Your opinion is not of interest to anyone, I say.

He laughs. Well, I'm off to give Frank Jr. the news that his mother is settled in her new home.

I wonder at your devotion to that boy, I say.

It's not for Frank Jr. particularly, he says, but for Mrs. Johnson and Lorna. Lorna and I were in the same grade at school, and she helped me get past algebra. We were friends, just that. It was terrible what happened to her. I helped Mrs. Johnson through it.

He leans into the pickup cab through the open passenger-side window. Has she ever mentioned any details of that difficult time to you?

He says this as if inviting a new conversation altogether and waits for my answer.

But I have no time for any sideshow of the chicken-lawyer's. It does seem that you have your hand in everybody's affairs, I say, and turn the engine on.

You'd sure make my job easier if you could give a straight answer now and then, he says, and pulls back out of the cab. But I guess it's not in your character. The fact is I'm on retainer with Frank Jr. until the sale of Mesa Portales to the BLM is done. As you once remarked, there's not a lot of lawyer work to be had around here, and I don't want to upset any steady customers.

Well, do your job and inform him that my lawyer will not be slow to act if there is any trespassing at Mesa Portales, I say.

The chicken-lawyer shakes his head. He'd be staying away to humor you, not because he doesn't have the right. But to avoid trouble I'll make sure he heads home and not to Mesa Portales. First I'll have to get some coffee in him.

One more thing, I say. The folks in Taos said no visitors for two weeks, to help Alice settle in. Those are the rules.

Why, I don't think Mrs. Johnson will like that, the chicken-lawyer says. She'll get lonely without familiar people around. Seems to me that'd produce the opposite effect.

I don't make the rules, I say. But I will pass along your concerns when I drop off Alice's things. We all of us want this to go smoothly.

I smile and nod when I am finished saying these things, which confuses him, but in the end he nods in return, gets in his car, and drives off down the road toward Alice's place.

With both Frank Jr. and the chicken-lawyer at Alice's, my business there will have to wait. Anyway, now I have new business in Taos. But I don't want to drive up there by myself, brooding over my situation. I look over at Veronica, still waiting on the curb, her arms wrapped tightly around herself.

Veronica, I shout. I'll give you a ride home after all.

She jumps up immediately, hustles over, and opens the passenger-side door, as if afraid I'll change my mind.

We'll stop in Taos on the way, I say.

She hesitates. Taos is not on the way.

I've had a change of heart, I say. Perhaps you were right about Alice being too much for me to manage at Mesa Portales. I've decided to inspect the place in Taos on her behalf.

Veronica is surprised, but her expression quickly changes to smug sympathy. You're doing the right thing, Agatha. But won't Alice want to see it for herself?

She trusts my opinion entirely, I say. Wait for the bus if you prefer. But the bus is slow. I'll get you back home sooner than that, even with the stop in Taos.

Still she hesitates! It is beyond belief that a baby might be more tempting.

Have a little spirit, I say. A grown man can change a diaper.

A bit of spark comes back into her. All right, she says. Hold on a minute.

She darts into the market without waiting for me to reply, and as if on cue the postmistress pops out of the post office, crosses the street, and presents herself at my window. For the first time in our acquaintance, her face is not open and lively. In fact it is nearly creased shut with worry.

Can you tell Alice I've got something for her, she says. She doesn't answer her phone.

Just give it to me, I say. I'll pass it on to her.

No, she says. There's a package. A *package*. Say it to her just like that. You know what I mean.

I don't know what you mean, I say, annoyed.

The postmistress leans in through the open window. I went out to her place yesterday looking for her, she says in a low voice. What in hell is going on out there? Lorna's grave is looking terrible! I did what I could and I did a good job of it, but you better make sure it gets watered twice a day or it'll go brown around the edges in this heat. We don't need this kind of trouble.

I am not often taken by surprise. Of course only the postmistress could have fixed up Lorna's grave so beautifully. But though I appreciate that she can't abide a garden mess and has therefore covered up my tracks, neither do I like her in my business.

I open my mouth to tell her this, but now Veronica is coming out of the market and I want no more discussion of the grave.

Why didn't you just leave the package when you were out there yesterday? I say. Alice isn't feeling well these days. Just give me this package and there will be no problem.

At this the postmistress steps away from the pickup, as if surprised. Good Lord, she says.

Good Lord what? I say, irritated.

I thought you said she'd talked to you about Lorna! The postmistress glances at Veronica. You tell Alice to come see me, she hisses, or have her call me. You tell her I need to talk to her. Don't forget, all right? Dial the number and hand her the phone. Tell her it's important.

Veronica slides into the passenger seat, holds a small bag of ice to her breast.

Almost forgot, the postmistress says to me in a regular voice. Your lawyer's called twice and wants you to get back to him pronto. He says it's about your lease.

I put the engine into gear. The postmistress steps back, and I watch her in the rearview until she turns back toward the post office.

Veronica shifts the bag of ice to her other breast. What was that all about?

People around here haven't anything better to do than bother old ladies, I say. It's a great entertainment for them.

But the surprise in the postmistress's voice echoes in my head: *Good Lord. Good Lord. Good Lord.*

13

W E DRIVE NORTH TOWARD TAOS, through Gallina and Coyote and on to Abiquiú, past cottonwoods along the river and orchards laid out below striped mesas. Now and then a car passes by from the opposite direction, a flash of teeth and a finger raised off the steering wheel in greeting.

Veronica stares out the window, her gaze drifting back and leaping forward, over and over. It's not possible to keep your eyes steady while looking at the world. She rolls the window down, flings away the ice now melted down to water.

That's better, she says, touching her breasts gently and wincing.

I keep my eyes on the road.

I talked to Dan, she says. They gave Margot a bottle last night when I didn't come back. They said she didn't mind, Margot didn't, that she accepted the bottle.

So it didn't miss you, I say to cheer her. It's good for it to start learning independence as soon as possible.

Babies can't be independent, she says.

Heavens no. But now that you've begun to separate, why not make a clean break? I've heard that formula is healthier for a baby anyway.

She throws me a dark look, very dark for Veronica, and makes a noise not quite a laugh. Where would you have heard that?

I'm trying to help you with your problem, I say.

The last time you tried to help me with my problem, she says, I didn't take your advice and I'm glad I didn't.

I suppose you never wanted my advice in the first place.

Being a mother is a big mistake, she says. That's what you think.

It's your life. I feel magnanimous when I say this to her. But you are mistaken if you think that it is just one choice you have made. In fact you have made a thousand. It's best to face these things so they don't swamp you.

We stop at Bode's for gas and a Coca-Cola. Across the road but up the hill and hidden from sight is Georgia's Abiquiú house. I once took Veronica and Dan there to meet her, and they didn't fawn, there was absolutely no fawning, they spoke intelligently, and I was proud of them. Veronica often hints around at seeing Georgia again, but already this baby has changed things; though we are only a stone's throw from Georgia, Veronica doesn't glance in the direction of her house. Instead she sags against the pickup as I pump the gas.

This is the longest I've ever been away from Margot, she says. She's three months old today. I'm so tired all the time. She rests her Coca-Cola bottle on the pickup hood, as if even its weight is too much for her.

I didn't hear a word from you for months, I say. I wondered what had become of you. I imagined that if you had died during a procedure, Dan would have informed me.

Veronica straightens up slightly. I was afraid to tell you that I was having the baby. I made Dan promise not to say anything.

When the pair of them came to Mesa Portales eight months ago, Veronica had cried and Dan stood with his hands in his pockets, watching her. This was not the sort of visit I had expected and I was angry with them both. I don't know what to do, Veronica had said, and I took that as a question that needed answering. I told her what to do, and she disregarded my advice. It is a hard lesson for both of us.

Well, how do you propose to carry on? I am cross when I say this. And what about Dan, have there been repercussions for him at the university?

Unlikely, she says.

Well, that is good news.

The department is advertising for an associate professor, she says. The dissertation may help. A recommendation from you would help as well.

It's unlikely that you'll be able to stay at the university, I say. A good solution would be to let Dan and Melinda have the baby. They have two already, it would have playmates.

She startles at my words. *No,* she says, in a tone I haven't heard from her before. I'm keeping Margot.

That's very foolish, I say.

We get back in the pickup and Veronica stares out the window. She is silent but her mind is working, thinking about how to get what she wants. She is so like a transparent child that it seems impossible that she has one of her own. It will rule her, no doubt.

But then she puts a hand on my arm.

Even before I told you about the baby, she says, you didn't seem quite yourself. It must be upsetting, what is happening with Alice.

I am affronted, because I am always myself. Though to hear Veronica say these words takes something out of me, even as I wonder if she is trying to distract me from her own problems.

I move my arm so her hand slips off. There is nothing I can do to help Alice anymore, I say. My voice rattles and echoes so loudly inside myself that I wonder if Veronica hears my emptiness. But she doesn't.

It's not true that you can't help her anymore! she says. Don't you think she'd enjoy meeting the baby? Unless that would upset her. No one in town will talk about what happened to her daughter.

Why didn't you ask me if you wanted to know? I say.

I know better than to ask you about Alice, she says.

Veronica knows very well why I don't answer questions about Alice, and it is because of Veronica's notebook, as Alice would not care to make an appearance in it.

But today is not the same as any other day, and perhaps it no longer matters whether I shield Alice from Veronica's notebook. So I tell Veronica the story of Lorna. She eats it up like candy.

Lorna was with the man from the armed robbery trial for three years. Alice never spoke this man's name, as if that would serve somehow to punish him. There were signs that he was no good, but he knew how to hide it. When Lorna rolled up her sleeves to help with the dishes or changed her shirt before Sunday dinner, Alice saw the marks. But Lorna denied it, turned away from Alice, and said that she loved the man, Like you love Pops.

One day the man shot Lorna. Alice never knew why or what led up to it. Afterward he went to jail, there was no technicality this time. Alice's husband went to the trial but didn't allow her to go, even though she got up early, was dressed and sitting in the pickup with her purse on her lap. She waited for the winter sun to come up, for her husband to take her to the courthouse.

But he took her by the arm and yanked her out of the pickup. It's too much for you, he said. She watched the pickup drive away. She screamed into the snowy morning and yanked out a handful of her own hair. But that was the most Alice ever did. She accepted things and did not try to change them.

What a terrible story, Veronica says, but she doesn't mean that she didn't like to hear it. In fact she is moved by this kind of story and it fills her with pity, a sensation most people enjoy and that they mistake in themselves for a sort of kindness.

14

THE TAOS SENIOR HOME IS a spruced-up boardinghouse not far from the plaza. It's true that Alice would enjoy the flowers planted in neat rows, the whitewashed gate and fence, the flagstone path. But these tidy things count for little when measured against the wild glory of Mesa Portales.

In the yard a dark-haired woman arranges dishes on a table in the shade of a crab apple tree. I don't call to the woman or introduce myself. I head straight for the front porch, where an old man sits on a chair. Veronica hurries to keep up.

I'm here to inspect the place, I say to the man.

He gestures vaguely toward the door while feasting his eyes on Veronica.

Should we check in with someone? Veronica peeks in a window.

Don't be ridiculous, I say. They'll just take the opportunity to pull the wool over our eyes about any deficiencies. Wait here if you want, but I'm going in.

The old man slides his hand in his pants.

I'll come with you, Veronica says.

Inside there isn't much to the place, just a long hallway with doors all down it, a dining room off to one side, and a staircase to the upper floor. It could be mistaken for a regular hotel if not for the handrails everywhere and the smell like days-old fatty stew.

I walk briskly toward a large window at the end of the hall. It is important to be brisk in this place, so as not to be mistaken for a person who lives here.

Overall I don't like this hallway. The walls are yellow and it's not a good yellow. Also the paint is smudged with handprints, as if the people who live here don't understand what a handrail is for or as if they frantically pat the walls hunting for a way out. All the doors have nameplates. Some doors are shut, some are open, and inside each room is a person. Eleanor Sandoval. Jarvis Purcell. Mariana Wilcox. There's a person with uncombed hair lounging on a bed. Another dozing in a chair. A man stares back at me, a towel draped over his shoulders, while a nurse-person shaves his whiskers. In one room a woman bares her teeth, and this gesture cheers me, its dark spontaneity.

At the end of the hallway is the window and outside it is a tree, an enormous flowering dogwood. In a storm it would be a powerful sight, its wet bare branches lashing against the glass.

Look, Veronica says. She stands close to me and points out the window into the distance. See the cemetery, there beyond the hedge and across the way? Very efficient, the proximity of it. She laughs.

But I feel laid low by the sight of it.

It's a joke, Veronica says when she sees my expression. You don't live here and it's got nothing to do with you. You're never going to die, Agatha.

I don't reply because I have noticed the nameplate on the door closest to the window. *Alcie Johnson.*

They spelled it wrong, Veronica says.

I turn the knob and go right in.

The room is empty, except for a bed and a nightstand, a soft chair and a desk. There are windows on two sides, one with a view of the mountains and the other of uninterrupted high desert. It's a lovely surprise after the dreadful hallway. But also I find myself disappointed. There is no quilt across the bed, no arrowheads or fossils or bud vase on the mantel, no coat on the hook. No brooch hidden in a clock. No Alice.

Veronica flops down into the chair. I think Alice will like it here, she says.

Now the room feels small and airless. Time to go, I say.

Right outside the door the dark-haired woman from the garden is waiting for us, arms crossed. May I help you. It's an accusation rather than a question. I admire her manner and also her firm tidy figure, her deep red lipstick, and lovely thick eyebrows. She smells of hot coffee. But I remind myself not to be distracted by her charms.

You've spelled the name on the door wrong, I say.

We did your name exactly like your son wrote it down for us, she says.

Haha!

The woman frowns and turns to Veronica. She wasn't expected until the day after tomorrow. We're not ready for her.

Veronica rightly stays quiet and looks down at her shoes, as this is not her business.

The woman turns back to me. You can't barge in here without asking first, she says. You don't live here yet. Come on outside now.

I'm not finished inspecting, I say.

She puts a hand briefly on my shoulder. I'm Francesca, she says. If you'd like to stay for lunch, I invite you. Ham sandwiches. Under the tree. We often eat out there.

She turns and walks down the hallway, her stride long and easy, a joy to watch. If a person were obliged to live in such a place, this woman would be a bright spot. She holds the door to the yard open, and there's nothing to do but walk through it.

We follow her to the picnic table under the tree, where three very old people sit. Francesca points to each one in turn, and while there is no reason to remember names, one is Rosa and one is Margery. The other one is a man.

I take the metal rocker on one end. In this way I am at the head of the table and at the same time not of it. Veronica sits down without a murmur. She is in full bloom among the wilting, the only one at the table able to sit up straight and tall. But there's no harm in a preview. Perhaps it will help her organize her thoughts about her own future, which are clearly in a jumble.

Francesca passes out sandwiches. This is Alcie Johnson, she announces. She'll be joining us permanently day after tomorrow.

Veronica meekly accepts a sandwich. I'm Veronica, she says to the table, too loudly, and smiles, too broadly.

Rosa winces. Is something wrong with your ears?

Margery pats Veronica's hand. We can hear you just fine, honey.

Everyone confronts their sandwich. There are murmurs and sighs and napkins unfolded. I approve of the way they lift the bread and take out what they don't like, the lettuce, the tomato, the ham. Rosa uses her long fingers to swipe the mayonnaise off the bread and plop it onto the ground. Margery cuts the crust off her bread and chops the sandwich into smaller squares with swats of a butter knife. The man covers the ham in a thick shower of salt, closes the sandwich back up, and eats without a grimace or a drink of water. Veronica gulps hers down in four bites and afterward glances around frantically for something more to do.

I eat my sandwich without modification and also slowly, because that is best for digestion.

What's all that paint? The man gestures at my overalls.

Agatha is an artist, Veronica says.

Who? Francesca asks sharply.

She means me, I say. Sometimes Veronica forgets things, like a person's proper name. She might need a room in a place like this sooner than she thinks.

All eyes turn to Veronica, who reddens.

Oh, now, she's a beautiful young girl, Rosa says. Her whole life ahead of her. Got a husband, honey?

Veronica shakes her head.

Well, she's got a baby, I say.

Veronica lifts her chin and takes out a picture from her purse. I pass it along without a glance.

Oh, what a darling! Margery says.

You must be a proud granny, Rosa says to me.

Ha! I say.

Alcie is a painter, Veronica says, and throws me a dirty look.

Hold on, the man says to me, are you that lady that lives in Abiquiú?

You mean Georgia O'Keeffe, Veronica says.

Flowers, Rosa says. Such pretty colors.

Laps, the man says.

This gets everyone's attention.

That's what the lady paints, he insists.

I'm not a lady, I say.

She's not Georgia O'Keeffe! Veronica says.

Laps! the old man insists.

You are being rude in polite company, Francesca says to him.

I guess I'll go on back to my room then, he says mildly, not in the least ashamed. I'm ready for a rest. He shambles off.

Francesca is frowning. Your son didn't mention painting, she says to me. We don't have that kind of thing here.

Is this Georgia a friend of yours? Margery asks me, hopefully. Will she come to lunch?

I consider this question. It's true that Georgia enjoys lunch and can always be counted on for a lovely one—buttermilk soup, locust flowers battered and fried in oil, green chile enchiladas—though there is never quite enough of it. On occasion she lectures me about my waistline, and in those moments I think of pie rather than argue, because she is the one person I don't care to rile up for just any reason. Though the last time I had lunch with Georgia, I had to take her aside and insist she never make Alice feel badly again. Why, nice was what Alice said about my own paintings! It is not important what Alice says about any paintings whatsoever; what is important is simply to appreciate the person that Alice is.

Georgia's face scrunched up sourly when I spoke sharply to her over this. Nothing set the luncheon right again, as all through it Alice talked and worried over her lost cane—even though in that moment the cane was not yet truly lost! In fact it was beside her chair and sometimes in her very hand, which Georgia noted with growing satisfaction. There is not an old person alive who does not appreciate the sight of someone frailer and less capable, and Georgia was no different. I saw the smugness come over her face and I did not like it. I said hard words to her, and we ended the day on bad terms. She followed us out to the patio, where Alice sat down on a bench next to the woodpile so that I could tie her shoe. Georgia and I both saw the cane slip down behind the woodpile with a quiet *clunk*; our eyes met, and then in silent agreement we both looked elsewhere. I took Alice by the arm and helped her to the car. I thought, Good riddance to that cane, and made no more mention of it.

Now, before I can answer the question as to whether Georgia would come to lunch at Alcie's new home in Taos, Rosa gestures dismissively with her hand.

Don't get anyone's hopes up by suggesting it, Margery! They always say they'll come visit but they don't. Anyway, I know about that Georgia, my friend's son works out at her place, and he told me what she gets up to. She has two houses and fancy cars and those dogs get their dirty paws all over everything.

That's true, I say, and tell them what Georgia likes to say about her dogs: I am a servant to them. Her dogs have eyes and snouts obscured by hair the color of soot or chrysanthemum, and she likes to brush these dogs until they are sleek and gleaming. In summer the dogs pant heavily, they suffer in the sun. There have been quite a few over the years. One was hit by a car and buried under a cedar tree; others died of old age. One disappeared entirely, and that was the worst for Georgia, because she didn't know its ending.

Margery bursts into tears from missing her own dead yellow dog, and this breaks up the lunch.

Francesca sternly suggests that everyone have some quiet time in their rooms. Rosa and Margery drift away, with Margery wiping her eyes. When Francesca carries dishes to the kitchen, I follow her. She sets the plates in the sink and turns to me, sighs as if expecting some kind of nonsense.

My son is a thorn in my side, I say. In fact I am hoping to be rid of him. If he comes around, I require that you send him away with no details, other than to tell him I am well but wish to be left alone to adjust to my new circumstances.

She raises her eyebrows. He demonstrated concern for your happiness and in fact insisted that you have the room with two windows, she says. He said you would need good light for your houseplants.

He must've been acting the good son, I say.

Relatives can be difficult, she says. It's more work for me to manage them.

I will pay twenty-five dollars extra per month, I say, but you must keep him out along with anyone else who comes around. Also I may move in later than expected, as I have many details to arrange. I will arrive when I am ready.

Your son paid for three months in advance, she says. Whether you arrive in two weeks or two months is your own concern. But I expect my first twenty-five dollars paid to me personally and up front.

We shake on it. Her fingers are warm but dry and don't give an inch.

I step back outside to get my wallet from the pickup's glove box and see Veronica chatting with the old man on the porch. He grins toothlessly at her, patting the seat next to him, beckoning. I watch her laugh and talk, making dramatic motions with her hands and asking him questions. I'm sure they're stupid questions, the kind most young people ask of an old person, as if humoring a wrinkled child.

Veronica is too busy jotting things down in her notebook to notice that I also take Alice's suitcase out of the pickup. I carry it down the hall to Alcie's room, slide it safely under the bed.

Then I give Francesca the cash. Now she smiles, folds it up, and slips it into her apron pocket. I watch her walk away, down the long hallway, until she turns the corner and disappears.

A few years ago in Marseille I left a gallery reception early, and on the walk back to my hotel I stopped to watch a clutch of children hunkered over a hole near the sea. The hole smoked and spat as the children threw sticks and rocks and scraps of things into it in the rhythm of a game they had made with rules I couldn't figure. An elderly beauty came out of a nearby house and showed me various things she had to sell: a flower-sprigged silk scarf, half a bottle of perfume, a pair of slightly worn green velvet slippers. I haggled with her for the slippers, and when I gave her the coins she smiled at me, the first true smile of that day, not of flattery or fatigue, but true in its delight for money. That was honest, that I could accept.

Francesca reminds me of that woman. I expect she rarely smiles, but when she does it is a picnic, a sunrise, an unexpected marvel. Ah, Francesca.

When I head back to the pickup, Veronica is still flirting with the old man. It is maddening that she sees a man and starts up with him, that in fact anyone ever does. Where do they think these things lead? Rarely anywhere good, only work without end and sometimes a prison in the shape of a backyard with a dead daughter buried in it. This happens anywhere you look in the world.

I start the engine and honk loudly. Veronica waves good-bye to the man, who blows her a kiss.

He is ninety-two years old, she says as she gets in the pickup. He has lived in Taos his whole life and went to parties at Mabel Dodge Luhan's house. Imagine! Maybe I should do an oral history with him.

She roots around in her bag, finds a pencil, and flips open her notebook.

You've been crying over being away from your baby, I say, but as soon as there's a dirty old man available, you dawdle with him.

He's not a dirty old man, she says.

It's terrible the way you carry on, I say. It's no way to get ahead in life. I hope this sort of thing isn't happening at the university. I wouldn't like that at all.

Veronica's face tightens. I know you think that's what happened with Dan! she says. But it wasn't like that, and anyway, it's not your business, and I'm not sorry because now I have Margot. What do you want, that I'm under your thumb for the rest of my life?

These last words of hers stop me cold. I get the pickup on the road and start driving in hopes of somehow leaving them behind us.

Veronica closes her notebook and puts the pencil behind her ear. She stares out the window. Why can't you understand that I am the one you can count on, Agatha?

15

VERONICA IS RUDE AND FALLS asleep on the drive. It's late afternoon when we reach the university neighborhood. I park in front of Dan's house.

Wake up, I say to Veronica.

She groans, but after all she has brought this situation on herself. She stumbles to the front door just as Melinda brings a bundle out to the porch. Veronica takes the bundle, and her face changes as she croons to it. Meanwhile the expression on Melinda's face is as sour as I feel, and we nod at each other from across the tidy lawn.

Then I honk and leave. Veronica turns in surprise as I pull away from the curb. But her apartment isn't far. She can easily walk. A walk is good for anyone. Anyway I don't want to meet the baby. What if it looks like Dan, and I find myself charmed by this evidence of their indifference to my opinion?

I park near the university and walk to the faculty offices. I like this campus, its modesty. The buildings are single-story stucco, and the sun keeps everyone quiet and hugging the strips of shadow along the edges of buildings. There is no suffocating ivy, and I can feel minds working, but not in the way of thinking too much, as they do in those places where people feel the need to be clever and are praised for it. I hope I've developed Veronica and Dan to be more than clever. But some days I have my doubts.

Now, arriving at Dan's office, I feel my spirits rise. There are students waiting in the hallway, but I go to the front of the line and walk right in. Dan puts aside his papers immediately. I don't beat around the bush in any way. What is all this about Veronica having the baby instead of fixing the situation, as I told them to do? What on earth was he thinking? What will happen now, with Veronica and the baby, with his reputation?

I am at my most severe because it's necessary for him to put things in order. There is no sense in shirking from the mess of life.

He winces and rubs his face with his hand. We've dealt with it the best we can. Everyone's been grown-up and understanding about it.

I suppose by everyone you mean Melinda, I say.

She has been good about it, he says. Far more so than I deserved.

Nonsense. Melinda is lucky to have you. But you have another responsibility and that's to Veronica.

There's nothing between us in that way.

Well, you can't let her life be ruined, I say. How can she move forward if she's saddled with a baby? You, on the other hand, have a wife and two children, and one more won't make a difference. Best for everyone.

Veronica won't agree to it, he says. And I'd have to talk to Melinda first.

You do that, I say. Talk to Melinda. Then the two of you talk to Veronica. It'll be hard for her in the short term, but she has a whole career ahead of her. It's not fair to take that away from her. And I won't let anyone take anything away from me.

Dan is always at his most mild when he means something forcefully. I have often admired this manner of his, but I don't like it when I hear his words and tone now.

I'm not taking anything away from Veronica, he says. And I don't see how it's a situation where anyone is taking anything away from you, Agatha.

We eye each other. I feel a hesitation in him that I can't put my finger on. I have to make him understand the rightness of the choice to claim the baby.

The truth is you can have the baby if you want it, I say. You're the father, and you have a job, a nice wife, a solid family life. What does Veronica have? There's likely no need for a lawyer. Things just need to be pointed out to everyone.

He makes a noise that might be yes or might be no. He takes a deep breath. Agatha, he says, are you all right?

The question is a dark distant bell, ringing.

We're here to discuss your problems, I say. I myself am perfectly fine. I'll have no nonsense from you today.

In the past Dan's nonsense has involved visits to a doctor and insisting I swallow a pill every morning. That nonsense made me feel not myself, and what was the point in that? I humored him for a time, but that's done now. I am the older and wiser person, after all.

Agatha, he says, has Julien started showing himself again?

No, I say. Not for years now, still.

Good, Dan says, relieved.

He's very far away, I say. In Norway.

Yes, Veronica told me you'd said that, Dan says.

And then we laugh—not a big laugh, only a very small one—because it makes things easier to bear. In the past we have often left his office and found a spot of shade to sit in on the grass outside, smoked a cigarette, and talked. But today I must keep moving only forward.

Well, give Melinda my best, I say.

And I leave him to mull over my advice about Veronica.

In the hallway the students look eagerly at me.

Ms. Smithson? A student comes forward, books clutched to her chest. I saw your lecture last spring. It was wonderful. In fact I'm writing a paper on your early works, the portraits.

You should drop that topic immediately, I say. I reject that early work of mine. In fact I've destroyed all of it that I can get my hands on. I don't believe it's possible to write a worthy paper on the subject of lesser work. Move to the highest level and set a bar, one that you refuse to go below.

She's crestfallen, poor dear, but I've never believed in babying anyone. It's not my job to make these children a success.

Regrettably that's all the time I can spare for them. I hear a low murmur of conversation in my wake. Undergraduates need excitement, and a brush with fame counts for something, especially in a backwater like this. And the truth is that in the end I might approve of such a research topic as the student spoke of, should it end with a description of my disavowal of it.

But my spirits drop once I get back in my pickup. My hands are on the steering wheel, but the keys are in my lap. I didn't ask Dan the question I most wanted him to answer, though it is also an answer I am afraid to hear. What good reason could he have for staying away so long? Nothing is like it used to be. Regarding Dan, I don't wish for things to move forward but to always stay the same.

16

LEAVE ALBUQUERQUE AND DRIVE NORTH. I banish thoughts of Veronica and Dan and their problems from my mind. But when I reach the turnoff for Mesa Portales, I keep going and continue on toward Ghost Ranch. I have not seen Georgia in some time, nor tried to.

Just past Abiquiú I see Pedernal, rising up a cool blue. Above the mountains, inside the brightest swatch of sky, are the clouds. These clouds are white and blithe, and they don't care a fig for anyone.

I turn onto Georgia's unmarked dirt road. The light has softened to a dull gold, and the smell of evening is thick with juniper and pine. When I see the house, low-slung and cradling the flagstone patio dotted with sagebrush, I feel a pull into the secret center of something. In fact this center is Georgia's will, a silent clang of intent that goes on occurring at every moment: everything is her way or the highway. But Georgia did not choose where her Ghost Ranch house was built, nor did she have a hand in making it; she only had the money to buy it. If she'd had a choice, she still would've placed it where it is now, at the foot of the hills, because in that way she is no different from most people. Not everyone is able to live the way I do.

I stop the car and peer across the patio toward the house, wait for Georgia to step outside. In summer she often wears a white head-scarf and loose dress, and I approve of this, her practicality. I myself would not dress in similar fashion, no matter how old I was, because I would resemble a member of the clergy and that would be distasteful to me. But that is not what Georgia brings to mind. Some people are made for clothing that photographs beautifully for magazines, and some people are best in overalls. Anyway, I have always been the dark horse.

Georgia does not appear. Instead a young man stands up from behind a clump of sagebrush where he has been crouched over, working. In his hand is a pair of small clippers, and on the flagstone path is an old blanket piled with sage tips.

Where's Georgia? I say.

Miss O'Keeffe is in Santa Fe seeing a doctor, he says. She's mostly at the Abiquiú house these days. I'm just here to do some maintenance.

I scowl, because is there a word more profane than *maintenance*? It is a living death. Nothing new can come into existence through unthinking habit.

The young man looks me up and down. You're Agatha Smithson, he says.

It seems he is an art lover as well as the torturer of wild sage. I head toward the woodpile without replying. He watches as I bend down to peer into the slip of empty space between the firewood and the adobe wall. I close one eye and squint.

What are you doing? the young man asks, agitated, now directly behind me.

I try to reach behind the woodpile, but my forearm is too thick. I start unstacking the wood, to get a better angle.

Let me do it, he says, stretching out his arm to stop me. Miss O'Keeffe likes her wood stacked a certain way.

I shift slightly to block him. I know how she likes it, I say.

Now I can reach down and grab the cane. It is dusty and cool, worn to a sheen from hands grasping it.

Is that Miss O'Keeffe's? he asks suspiciously.

I say nothing, only restack the wood with care, all facing-out ends of the wood even with one another. He may wonder if I have come to steal a cane that is dear to Georgia, but also he knows that I am Agatha Smithson. He is paralyzed between these two ideas. Well, I won't help him.

I swing the cane over my shoulder and walk back to the pickup. You can tell Georgia I came to get Alice's cane, I say.

But he follows me. I suppose you've heard about her macular degeneration, he says, as if to surprise me with his intimate knowledge of Georgia.

I stop walking and stand utterly still. The smell of sage is overpowering. A bird trills then cuts off abruptly. In fact I had not heard this terrible news.

She can only see out of her peripheral vision now, he says. It's difficult for her to paint. But I'm a potter, and I've started showing her how to work with clay. It keeps her spirits up, to work with her hands.

He says these things self-importantly and waits to hear what I will say. Perhaps he has his own notebook near at hand, ready to memorialize the moment that Agatha Smithson learned that Georgia

O'Keeffe is going blind. I can sense the strong beat of his blood, his future stretching out before him, his eagerness to overtake us.

I get back in my pickup and lay the cane on the seat beside me.

Please tell Georgia hello from me, I tell him, and also that I am thinking of her.

I make sure to drive off in such a way that the young man disappears in a cloud of dust. The cane doesn't jostle and bounce along the rough road out of Ghost Ranch; instead it stays perfectly still on the seat, with a kind of matchless and malevolent gravity. I will never be rid of the shame of it.

There is no mystery to this cane, which is of dark varnished walnut, plain, with a well-turned handle. It is a cane like any other, and I myself bought it for Alice off a man sitting near the chapel in Chimayo, where we had gone on a Sunday drive. Alice's gait that day was uncertain, I could see that she needed steadying, and when I returned with the cane she looked up from the bench where I'd settled her. I saw her color rise at the sight of me; she smiled mischievously and winked. This wink brought me back to earlier days.

I presented her with the cane, and she said, Let's give it a whirl. We walked around the outside of the chapel three times as she practiced with it, and when we stopped at the chapel gate near the rosebushes she laughed and put a hand on my arm. I guess we're married now, she said, an honest pair!

Over time she often forgot how she came to have the cane, but she always remembered me inside that same space of forgetfulness. Once I found her crying on the porch because she couldn't remember what it was she wanted. I offered suggestions: the watering can, her navy-blue cardigan, a stamp for the phone bill. Only when I picked the cane up off the backyard grass and brought it to her did she light up. Oh, she said, exactly how this thing turns on I can't remember, but I know you love me.

It was wrong to leave it behind the woodpile when it fell unnoticed. Georgia had been cruel that day, Alice had been flustered, and I was angry and irritable with them both. I wanted to never hear a word about that cane again, nor witness Georgia's ill-disguised enjoyment over it. In that bad moment I wanted to be on the side of Georgia, on the side of strength and clarity, because I resented Alice's weakness and the suffering it caused inside me. When my eyes met Georgia's over the fallen cane, I was briefly consoled.

I thought Alice would forget about the cane once it was gone and that my sadness and anger would ebb. Instead her worry over the cane became a distressed and frantic drumbeat that never stopped. She drove everyone to exasperation until they refused to believe in the cane at all.

But the cane is real and does exist. In that way it is no different from my love for her, and in her head they had become the same. Yet I let her imagine that it was gone because I was afraid and angry. I wonder if she can ever forgive me.

TWO

1

I T IS HARD TO LOSE a true friend. There are so few of them. I am not a lonely person. I can call my shark-lawyer, my gallerist, Veronica, Dan. My university students often left gifts and notes outside my office door. I go to cities all over the world and everyone applauds. I am not exaggerating when I say these things. But there is little that I want from any of them.

Alice was different. She knew about sitting quietly in a backyard with her dead daughter. She knew when everything began to dim. She would say, Let's pick a sprig of mint for your iced tea, and lead me to the wild patch of it, gripping my hand to steady herself as she picked it. But always I was the one steadied. All other lives were very far away when I was with her.

Just two weeks ago there was a morning with her at the Del Prado. As we waited for a table she pressed her chest with a trembling hand.

There's dirt caught in my throat, she said, gasping. Big clumps!

I patted her gently on the back and got her a glass of water. I told her to swallow; I told her to breathe deeply. We locked eyes until she calmed.

When people stopped by our booth to say hello, she tried to hide

her confusion with a smile so dazzling and practiced that until recently it had fooled even me. But after Hello, how are you, can you get
over this weather? she did not know what more to say.

I tried to make up for her uncertainty. I took her hand across the
table. I stopped her from pouring syrup in her coffee. I ordered her
breakfast and I insisted that she eat.

People watched all this, how I, her greatest friend, was caring
for her.

A young woman, a student from the handful of years Alice was a
math aide at the school, came up to our booth. She had a baby with
her. It was in a carrier. She held the carrier up to show Alice the baby.
Alice was delighted. She waggled her fingers and said, What a beautiful baby! What a beautiful baby!

I shifted toward the window so the heat of this young woman
could slide in next to me, across from Alice. She placed the carrier
with the baby in it on the floor next to the booth.

Alice listened to her talk and nodded along, saying, Oh my.
Well, what a thing. Yes, of course. But gradually understanding
came over the young woman. Her face grew disappointed in and
pitying of her old math aide, as people her age do when they ob-
serve their elders failing. The young woman's monologue trailed
off, and for need of something else to do she leaned down to chuck
her baby under the chin. Alice looked over and beamed excitedly
as if seeing the baby for the first time. What a beautiful baby! What
a beautiful baby!

This happened again, and then again. The baby could not be held
in Alice's brain. To me this was reasonable. The baby was not import-

ant to her. She had no need to remember it. What she needed was to keep hold of significant things and let everything else fall away.

At first the young woman tried to remind Alice that she'd already met the baby. As if a particular baby had special qualities that everyone would remember! The young woman's lips pursed in distress, and she drummed her fingers on the table and jittered her knee. I knew she was thinking of how to get away. I wouldn't help her. This young woman was acting like a child herself, in my opinion.

Stop trying to correct her, I said. She is enjoying seeing the baby and would a hundred times over. Why would you interfere with her pleasure?

It cost the young woman to take my advice, I could see that. Are you her helper? She whispered this to me as Alice began another round of What a beautiful baby!

Do I look like a nanny to you? I said this with an even-handed civility that confused her.

The young woman waited for more, but I felt no need to speak again, because who was she to me? She was no longer even anyone to Alice.

Then a young man joined us. Alice lit up in a way that made me think she recognized him, that he must also have been her student at one time.

But she didn't know him at all. It was simply that he was a man.

The young woman introduced him as her husband. Alice held out her hand coyly to him. She was in fact flirtatious. It was a ghastly pantomime, and I could not bear to watch. Maybe this was how she spoke to her future husband when she was fourteen years old and waiting tables in this very diner, flirting with him all the way until her fifteenth birthday, when she walked down the arroyo in the dark to marry him. I'd never liked the thought of that, and I didn't like to watch Alice flirting with this unremarkable person now.

The young man was amused by Alice. He flirted gently back. Who's your friend? he asked, and gestured in my direction.

When Alice turned her coquettish smile on me, her face faltered. She opened her mouth and shut it. Why, I don't know, she said to the young man. Do you know?

I was flooded with anger and upset. I shouted for the check. I pounded the open flat of my hand on the table when the waitress didn't hurry. The young woman turned away from me and picked up her baby.

Oh, what a beautiful baby! Alice clasped her hands together. Whose is it?

I thought wildly of all the reasons that I must never lose her. If she left me, if she flew away like a bird, so high and far away that I was obscured by distance—oh, I would die, or want to.

I paid the bill and helped Alice arrange her pocketbook strap into the crook of her elbow. Back outside I opened the pickup door, eased her into her seat and buckled her seat belt, squeezed her hand. Her eyes followed me as I walked around the front of the pickup and got in behind the wheel. When I pulled the door shut, we were once again in our own quiet. We sat and watched the people in booths talking, eating, squinting in the sun that shone in on them through the windows.

I waited for Alice.

After a while she put a hand on my arm.

I'm tired, Aggie, she said. Let's go home.

Every day I keep moving forward, as if we always will. I will not allow that she is headed to the place where we are all headed one day.

THE POSTMISTRESS WAS ALSO AT the diner that day two weeks ago. I'd spotted her at the corner table as we came in. She waved hello with her cigarette hand, smoke looping around her. I was suspicious to see her, as she was a regular at the other diner in town. I steered Alice across the dining room and settled her into a booth with her back to the postmistress.

I kept an eye out while I helped Alice with her coffee, and when the postmistress got up from her table to come over, I thought about what I might say to her. Lately it had come over me more clearly that the postmistress and Alice had a secret current of understanding between them. I did not know the quality of this understanding, but there was a measure of tenderness in it and I did not want to know its source; I only wanted it to dry up and disappear. There was so little of Alice these days. If the postmistress came over to our table I would not put up with it, I would demand that she be on her way.

But in the end I did not demand anything, because the young woman with the baby appeared and the postmistress turned back to her own table, lit another cigarette, and asked for more coffee. The postmistress was a person who could be patient.

Later, when Alice and I left the restaurant in a fuss and in a hurry, I didn't think of the postmistress. But as we sat in my pickup outside the diner and waited for Alice to return, the postmistress appeared. She reached in through the open passenger-side window and took Alice's hands in her own, gently squeezed.

Alice, she murmured. She murmured this as if I weren't there! Alice, what about Lorna?

Alice bent her head down and kissed the postmistress's knuckles. The shock of this froze me in my seat.

Lorna passed, Alice said, her voice breaking. I'm sure sorry if I forgot to tell you. I can't keep track of much these days. She's buried in my own backyard.

The postmistress shook her head. Come on, Alice, think.

But Alice disengaged her hands from the postmistress's grasp. Come on by the house and I'll show you Lorna's grave, she said. Promise you'll come by? Agatha will make us iced tea, won't you, Agatha?

She put her hands over her face and began to cry.

Oh, honey, the postmistress said.

At *honey* I leaned across the seat toward the postmistress. What game are you playing at? I asked.

But the postmistress ignored me, only leaned in to kiss Alice on the cheek before stepping away. Don't you worry, she said to Alice. Don't you worry.

2

A FTER THAT DAY AT THE Del Prado, Alice rarely spoke. At first I imagined she was thinking things, and I waited for her to tell me what those things were. But she was just drifting off to a place only she could go.

Only once did she pause from this drifting and lift her head to tell me that after Lorna had moved away to Albuquerque, the Navajo boy married a new sweetheart. He came by Alice's house with his bride, she with the loveliest eyes Alice had ever seen. The boy's face had become stern, and he newly had the feel of a man about him. He thrust a photo into Alice's hand. In the photo neither he nor his bride is smiling, but even so it's a happy photo. Alice never showed it to Lorna, though she knew that's what the Navajo boy wanted her to do.

Later Alice heard that they had a child, then a few more; that one child won the state spelling bee and went away to college back east. After that the family moved to Arizona and she didn't hear anything more about them.

They'd loved each other since they were children, Alice said. I lost Lorna all over again when I lost track of him.

She wrung her hands.

Now I forget and I remember that Lorna is dead, she said. I forget and I remember. It is too much, it is too much, Agatha, and I won't do it anymore, it is too much coming and going for one person. It is death every day. It is too much.

I put my arm around her, I did my best to comfort her. More than ever I imagined her at Mesa Portales, where she could leave some things behind.

3

F OUR DAYS AGO WAS THE day that I insisted Alice move up to Mesa Portales with me.

I chose an hour very dear to me, summer afternoon. Alice rested in the chair facing Lorna's grave. I sat down next to her.

A note was taped to Lorna's cross, written in Alice's spidery hand: *my Daughter.*

I did feel a tightness in my chest at that. When she saw me reading the note, her smile dimmed. She looked at me with sadness and also with shame.

It's all right, I said. It's all right.

I touched her arm.

Alice, I said.

I took her hand.

Alice.

She turned her lovely eyes to me.

I explained it so she would understand. I included important details: my pickup's flatbed, my strong arms and sturdy shovel, the perfect spot not far from the ledge at Mesa Portales, so that Lorna will still be near.

Come live with me and be my love, I said. No one will think it of us two old birds.

She smiled and squeezed my hand.

I squeezed her hand in return, relieved.

Yet again she shook her head! No, she said, because what will happen to Lorna?

She asked for iced tea and I went inside to make it. I took the carton of milk off the bookshelf and put it back in the refrigerator. *Car keys on hook. Water plants. Comb hair.* I threw away some old magazines on the counter because she wouldn't miss them, and they were an affront to an orderly mind. I chipped ice and made two tall glasses of tea with lemon and sugar. I took up a glass in each hand and turned back toward the yard. I would try again.

There have been moments in my life after which nothing has been the same. Now here was another one.

I took the step off the back porch slowly, because I'm portly in the way of old men and my tread is heavy. But my eyesight is excellent, and the instant I glanced at Alice, I knew that she had gone.

She did not look up and smile as she usually did. She did not say, Thank you, sweetheart. Instead her head was nodded slightly down and her eyes were directed vacantly at her hand in her lap. Her other hand—could it still be called hers?—it hung slack at her side with nothing to do.

I tried to pretend that this thing had not occurred.

I said loudly, firmly, Here we are.

I held a glass of iced tea out to her.

But Alice didn't lift her hand to take the glass, she didn't move or speak, and so I didn't either.

This was the terrible void. It was impossible to breathe inside of it. This void was not a thing of my imagination; instead it was the truest thing I had ever known. I recognized it but could not comprehend it. It was the world anew, now dark and empty.

I stood with the glass of iced tea held out, until my arm began to shake. I bent over and put both glasses down on the path. I became cold and my teeth chattered, and I said to myself, *Breathe!* because I want always to live. At first my chest did not rise and I had no air. But I tried again and this time succeeded. My skin flushed and tingled with heat. I, Agatha, I was alive.

But not Alice. Her body was there in front of me, but she was not. There was no more to her, nor would there ever be. Death was real and I could not stop it. I am sixty-eight years old, and before that moment I had not allowed death any purchase. It was a long time to deceive myself.

A noise came out of my mouth, a noise I would not wish anyone else to hear me make. We are all of us hunted animals from the moment we are born.

I SAT OPPOSITE HER FOR some time. Most days we shifted the positions of our chairs as afternoon and evening passed, to keep the sun off our faces. But on that day its last rays burned down on both of us. I suffered it gladly as a distraction. I wondered, Is sunburn possible after death?

I sat as if stone. My breath was shallow, my hands were cold. The world was silent. I was afraid that I would never hear anything again. But after some amount of time sounds came back into me. The birds. A rustle of dry leaves. The buzz of a dragonfly, and a car passing on the road.

And I felt a fury at the birds and the leaves, the dragonfly and the cars that passed on the road, all of them marking the passing of time that took me further and further from Alice. Here was the clock, here was the knock on the door.

I had a few other thoughts. Some were fearful and sad to me, and so I pushed them aside. Other thoughts were angry. One thought was that Alice did not try hard enough to dodge her death. She was so often mild. She did not fight things. She accepted them, whether it was a scolding or a slap. Death came for her, and I suspect that she did not fight to stay with me.

Her face was taking on the quality and appearance of the rubber gloves she put on every evening for washing up, to save her hands. I stared at each feature of her face, her lips in particular, until in death their shape became alien to me, simply forms in the landscape, so that I could not recognize my desire in them. I watched the skin that covered her face thicken because her heart no longer pumped, and I saw how gravity tugged her blood down into her ankles.

Oh, I was afraid! I was afraid to look upon her, dead; yet there she was.

Oh, my dear, I said.

Of course she did not answer, she never would again.

◆　　◆　　◆

IT HAD BEEN A LONG time since I had recalled my childhood. My mother, my sister, my brother; the grassy prairie that met a severe horizon and the long road that had stretched away from it. But when I looked at Alice, I remembered. There is no way to comprehend the opposite of living; it is only natural to think back and hope for a glimpse at how we ever began at all. But there was no answer to this, and Alice had disappeared into all the other mysteries.

Alice was dead. What would she think of that?

But she could think nothing whatsoever of her own death; it was impossible that she could do so. She would never think or laugh or stand in all her naked beauty under a bright sun. She would never want or wish anything for herself again.

THE EVENING CAME AND PASSED; the light dimmed. There was a breeze and the hint of a thunderstorm to come. I observed myself. I thought a few thoughts on my own behalf. It was true that Alice had once looked at Frank Sr. and thought, *Husband.* That was the road offered and she took it. But that was before she knew me. Now let him wait for her in the cemetery for all eternity.

I would not make a phone call, drive into town, attend a funeral. I would not let the family and town take over, because it would be Frank Jr. taking over, it would be the chicken-lawyer taking over. They would bury Alice next to her dead husband in the Presbyterian cemetery and likely move Lorna alongside them.

That would be the normal way of things, and no one would argue against it.

Except for me. I would argue against it, I would not agree to it.

I am quick to recognize the correct path forward in all situations, and this was no different. The only way out of this situation was through action, and so I stood up as resolutely as I was able.

In that exact moment, as if I had upset the universe with my resolve, Alice's body fell forward onto Lorna's grave, a slow-motion topple that picked up velocity as her muscles offered no resistance against the weight of themselves, the weight of Alice. She landed in a careless heavy heap across Lorna's grave.

I shrieked. I clapped a hand over my mouth. I felt like a foolish person, one with whom I would not want to be acquainted. I stumbled back. I looked around wildly as if a crime had been committed and I would be accused of it. In fact a crime had been committed, though not by me. It was just the world, and nothing less.

I BURIED ALICE BEHIND THE lilacs where Lorna used to play. I dug the grave only two feet deep because I could not manage more, and anyway, it was temporary. The lilac roots were dense and twisted, I hacked each shovelful from the earth. I worked in a frenzy because I did not want anyone to come upon me. Later I would think of the empty grave up at Mesa Portales, already dug and ready for Lorna; but in those early hours I was not thinking of practicalities. I only wanted the shovel in my hands and to know that I was still alive and vigorous. I did not want to think at all. But I could not stop myself from moaning out loud.

When I finished I went inside and took Alice's favorite sheet from her bed, the pale blue one with the yellow daisies. I spread it out on the ground.

The next part was very hard. I wrapped her up tenderly. In death her lovely fingers had clenched. The nails on one hand were bitten to the quick, while those on the other were filed neatly. All her life people had tried to make her stop biting her nails, including methods such as hitting, lye, and no dinner. But she didn't care to give it up, the habit of it comforted her, so she kept her right hand nicely trimmed but her left one in her pocket. With me she didn't hide it, and I was accustomed to seeing her left hand as often as her right.

I pressed her hands on her chest and hid them under a bouquet of flowers from her garden. Cosmo, sunflower, sweet pea.

Then I pulled the sheet across her and she was gone.

4

THE MORNING AFTER I TAKE Veronica back to Albuquerque, I
drive to Josey's house and honk the horn. His mother appears in
a housedress, white cotton with red flowers.

What do you want, Agatha? she says.

I'm here for Josey.

She crosses her arms. He can't help you anymore. He's going to be
busy with school.

His mother has helped make Josey the boy he is, and I appreciate
that. But I do not appreciate having to chat with her about things that
are obvious. All the same I take care to be polite.

Did you know I used to be a schoolteacher? I say. I can teach Josey
what he needs to know. I could spend an hour a day with him, and he'd
learn more than in a year in the classroom.

Josey's mother laughs but with no humor. There's no call for him
to be a painter, she says.

It's not about painting, I say. It's about how to see things. It's about
an approach to the world. He doesn't have to want to be a painter for
me to educate him properly.

Josey knows a lot about the world already, she says, maybe more than a kid his age should. He needs some school is what he needs. With other kids. He can't spend all his time with an older lady who isn't his family. It's not natural. He can't come out to help you anymore and that's final. If you're a teacher like you say, well, I'm sure you'll understand that.

I look away from her. Benighted people and their defenseless children.

Josey has come out to the porch and hears the last bit of our talk. Behind his mother he nods at me, firmly. When she turns back toward the house, I nod in reply.

I PULL THE PICKUP UP to Alice's lilac bushes. I think of Josey's desire for Lorna to be in a coffin, and my resolve falters. But I pick up the shovel and start digging, because there is a job to do, and after all, this is not my first exhumation.

I dig until I see the blue sheet with the yellow daisies, and then I slow down. Not long ago, Alice wept: Everything is so close, but also everything has gone so far away! At the time her words sounded like nonsense to me, and I disregarded them. But now I remember them with pain.

I gently brush the dirt away with my fingers because I don't want the shovel to touch Alice. When her swaddled outline is clear, I turn my face away because I am frightened. I do not want death in my mouth, down my throat, forcing its way into my lungs.

And yet it is Alice that I am avoiding, it is her dear body.

I hold my breath and gather her into my arms. She is stiff, and it is difficult. This is still Alice, I tell myself, even though in every way that matters I know that it is not. What I feel most fiercely is that I will allow no one to take her body from me.

I stagger toward the pickup. I lean on the lowered tailgate to steady myself as I ease Alice into the pickup bed. The arrangement of her distresses me, her crooked posture. I try to adjust her here and there, her shoulder, her knee. But as she is unforgiving, and it is impossible to be gentle and at the same time successful in this endeavor, I stop and leave her as she is. I tuck a tarp over her, so that she can't be seen by anyone, and close the tailgate.

Next I turn my attention to the yard. There is less to worry over than with Lorna's grave, as Alice was sheltered by the lilacs and hidden from view. I quickly fill in the hole and spread leaves and sticks across the top.

After that I sag down into my usual chair by Lorna's grave. As the postmistress predicted, her beautifying work could not hold forever, and the grave is no longer pristine. A thin line of brown grass now roughly outlines the grave, and irregular patchwork bits show through here and there across the mound, where our shovels chopped it into pieces.

Yet when I hear Frank Jr.'s truck, I feel not the slightest concern. In fact I laugh, as he is a bad refrain that repeats too often. Also I feel only an unholy confidence because the worst thing has already occurred. Alice is dead. Nothing will ever be so bad or of such importance again.

I heave myself up and go into the house through the back door. I take Alice's smock off the peg in the bathroom and pull it down over my overalls to cover up the dirt smudged all over me. The smock, so loose on Alice, is a tight fit, and my purse of letters bulges out in high relief from my middle. I take Alice's rubber gloves from alongside the kitchen sink and tug them on.

Now I need only be myself. I step out onto the front porch, as if I have been inside all this time.

Why are you here again, for chrissakes? Frank Jr.'s clothes are rumpled and his face sags.

Your mother asked me to water things in her yard, I say. When I got here, I found a mess inside. I'm tidying up a bit.

My lawyer said it's thanks to you she got up to Taos without a fuss, he says grudgingly. Also I heard that you might be persuaded to make me an offer for Mesa Portales.

You heard wrong, I say. I have a lifetime lease and therefore have no need to purchase it.

Either I'm kicking you off the place, he says, or Uncle Sam will.

I'm not leaving, I say. My own lawyer will see to that.

I walk toward my pickup without removing the smock or gloves, as I want to be gone from here before he gets a good look at what's in my flatbed.

But he shouts after me. If you're so eager to help out around here, I could use an extra pair of hands to move Lorna. No reason to wait now that Ma's in Taos.

It is a gift of mine to think quickly on my feet, and it does not fail me.

Well, someone may have beaten you to it, I say. It looks like the grave has been messed with. It's hard to say if Lorna is still there or not.

Frank Jr. stares at me, then strides off to the backyard. When he returns, his face is pale. Some person around here is sick in the head, he says.

Think about who you might've scared into action with your reckless intentions, I say with all the severity I can muster. The whole town knew you were digging that cemetery grave for Lorna, and I'm sure your mother heard about it. She doesn't want Lorna there. She wants Lorna always near her. You know very well she is having trouble thinking straight these days. You might have taken more care.

I allow time for his brain to catch up.

He paces around in a circle, takes off his hat, and runs a hand through his hair, agitated. Ma, he says. You think Ma tried to dig her up?

When his voice cracks, I feel a bit of shame. But I say nothing, not a word.

You really think Ma might've done that? I can't believe it.

He's struggling to keep his face still, but the longer I go without answering, the harder it is for him. When his chin begins to quiver, not even I can bear it. A strange keening howl comes out of him.

She's really lost it now, he says. Oh God!

There now, I say, and pat him awkwardly on the back, which is soft and trembling, and his shirt is damp with sweat. These things happen when folks get older.

He whips his head up to look at me. I never heard of a thing like this happening, he says. It's the worst I ever heard of.

Well, your mother's settled now, I say uneasily. I get in the pickup and pull the door shut, turn on the engine.

His eyes are wild. You're just going to leave, after all the talk about how you take care of my mother? What if Lorna isn't there anymore? How are you going to protect Ma from what she's done?

I have a new feeling, and it is the feeling of a guilty person. I close my eyes to clear this feeling, but it doesn't go away. When I open my eyes, I flinch at finding Frank Jr. right up next to me at the pickup window.

Don't you tell anyone about this! he says. You promise me that, right now.

I promise, I say.

He clutches his head. What would Ma have done with her if Lorna isn't there? he asks, despairing.

I have no more stomach for this story I've been spinning.

Your mother's not strong, I say. She couldn't have done much. Likely she had a bad moment, then came to her senses and tidied it back up. You just leave everything as it is back there for now, that's my advice, just let it all blow over. I'm sure Lorna is still there.

I'll have to talk to Ma about it, he says grimly. Just in case there's more to know.

He steps back from the pickup. Before he can widen his gaze to include the pickup bed, I point to the passenger seat.

Look what turned up, I say.

Christ, he says, is that the goddamn cane she was always on about?

I think of Alice's wink outside the chapel, her delighted smile as I presented her with the cane.

Yes, I say. The cane is real.

I don't waste the moment with his attention diverted from the flatbed. I step on the gas and drive away without a good-bye.

◆　◆　◆

BACK AT MESA PORTALES I release the tailgate.

I pull away the tarp and look down at Lorna's coffin. The grave is in no way a regulation depth. Who knew it would need to be deep enough for two? Only three feet of earth will shelter Alice and Lorna.

If I knew a prayer I would say it. Instead I gather Alice up and ease her down onto the ground alongside the grave. I squat down next to her and brace myself. I grab a fistful of flowered sheet in each hand and try to ease her over the grave so that I can let her gently down into it.

But my knees give out and the sheet slips from my hands. When she lands with a sudden thud on top of Lorna's coffin, I am not sure I can survive it. I freeze in place until the sound fades away, and then I look down at her.

Alice, my love, in a flowered sheet.

I turn away and sit down heavily on my stool. I look to the ocean canyon for relief but don't find it. The cat pushes itself up into my arms, and I stroke it until my breathing slows. I wrap my arms around it, too tightly, until it squirms out of my grasp and darts away.

I stand up again. I toss the rubber gloves and smock into the trash pile to be burned. I take my purse off and dangle it and Alice's letters over the grave. But then I change my mind and put the purse back on. Also I keep the cane.

I did not agree with the last letter Alice wrote to me. It was an argument we were having, and I believed that once up at Mesa Portales she would understand that I was the person who was right. Instead she died. It is no way to prevail, and so that last letter is unfinished business and cannot be buried. I fill the grave with dirt. Amen.

5

Dear Agatha,

Today I feel like myself. I made breakfast and it tasted right. I got dressed and tied my hair with the flowered scarf you like. The plants are watered and Lorna's grave is weeded. There is no better spot in the world than right here in my own backyard. For me that is true. I know you take a different view, and sometimes I like to be here alone, where I can enjoy things without feeling that you don't agree. Even when you manage to stay quiet about something, you are still plenty loud.

The hollyhock from Georgia's seedpod is coming up along the shed. By summer it will be dark purple and six feet at least. I haven't pointed it out because of your temper. Your reason for ending your friendship with Georgia is not right. It's true she can be sharp, but you are the same. If Georgia doesn't think I understand her paintings, it means nothing to me. A bit of hurt feelings is not lasting, or shouldn't be. You should forgive her because you will need your friends.

What is happening to me also happened to my mother, so I am not illusioned. It seems that some days I know it and some days I don't. It is a lonesome valley, one day I will walk into it and never come out again. I have a suffocating feeling in my chest over that, and also because of Lorna. It is all my fault, what happened. I am thinking about regrets in my life.

I am writing some things down because when I try to say them to you out loud, you argue as you do, and I forget my point. I hope what I am writing is clear. I can only try.

Agatha, you are not like anyone else, and I love that about you. I know you can only do things in your own way. Most days I appreciate that. You have strong ideas about what is right, but you forget that no two people agree about everything. Everyone is their own cowboy, as my husband used to say. That is one thing he said that I agreed with.

Here is what I want to tell you. You should not have built the house on Mesa Portales. This has been my opinion since Frank Sr. first told me about it. He didn't care what you did up there, all he cared for was the money he could get from you, and I knew better than to argue with him over it. I didn't want to argue with you either, and it was worth it to me to stay silent, in order to have you. But now I want to say it, before I can't anymore. That you put a house right on top of Mesa Portales was wrong and also it hurt me.

Agatha, do you imagine you are the only one to appreciate Mesa Portales? It has been in my family since before I was born. Before my family there were other families, and we sometimes found their pottery and arrowheads. But one summer, when I was still small, my mother let some university men dig up there, and they took it all away. Later we found out they lied about a museum, that the pottery and arrowheads were just in a drawer somewhere or sold to collectors.

My sister and I always took our birthday picnics there. One year she fell asleep in the sun, I brushed bits of grass from her hair and watched the thunderstorms cross the valley. I think my sister has been dead for some years now. My memories are very rich and sometimes it is hard to be sure.

I think I've told you that our father died when I was nine. After that my mother prized her tulip bed even more highly, as our father had given her the bulbs on their wedding day. She had planted them along the front porch and carried water from the creek, hoarded eggshells and coffee grounds like gold. Every year she had three weeks of springtime for her trouble.

Then one spring my aunt Honey from Pie Town came around with her husband and one small son, scruffy as an unwashed orphan. It is terrible, but I can't remember my little cousin's name and there is no one left to ask. My aunt's eyes were sad, her husband's hard as flint, and between them they filled up the room with misery. My mother said this misery was about being poor. But also Aunt Honey's husband was mean. We were also poor, but it didn't make us mean.

We suffered with him in the house. We never would call him Uncle. One day my sister pushed his dirty feet off the kitchen table. That dugout's surely dry by now, she said. Not Christian of you to begrudge us shelter, he said, and left his plate for her to clear.

Our mother said that Aunt Honey had a heavy cross and that she hoped we girls would always help each other like she was doing. But finally Mother took Aunt Honey down into the cellar for a talk. After that Aunt Honey put their belongings in an old feed sack and said to her husband, We got to go. He shoved the coffee table across the room with his foot and shouted for my cousin on his way out the door.

Aunt Honey touched Mother's cheek with her hand. Then the door opened and my cousin ran back in holding out a bouquet of tulips, all the stems bent and the petals dropping everywhere. He said, Daddy told me pick every last one. Then that poor child scuttled out.

The tulips drooped. They'd be on the compost by end of week. Mother's shoulders also drooped, but she arranged the tulips in a vase and we admired them during supper. Later she stepped out onto the porch and gave a cry at the sight of the empty tulip bed, its churned-up earth. My bulbs, she said, every last one.

My sister woke me at dawn the next day with a shake of my shoulder. We slipped out of the house and started hitching. The last few miles we rode in the back of a rattling cart with a family of five squeezed onto the front bench seat. The children turned their heads to stare at us.

At that time Pie Town was just a church that couldn't pay a minister and a café long out of everything. Aunt Honey saw us coming and stepped out onto the planks that passed for the porch. In Pie Town she was different, harder. She said, Girls, we ate them, all right? I cut them up for soup. Your mama will forgive me. We've got nothing.

Her husband saw us and said, Go on, git! We don't want you around here.

My sister said, It's not Christian of you to steal from us. You could've sold those bulbs and eaten for a month.

He said, No one's spending a dime on that fanciness, and it's a crime to waste the water on them. Now get out before I kick your tails to kingdom come.

After the door slammed we stared at three mugs drying on a dish towel in the sun. These mugs were tin cans with a bit of wire strung around for a handle.

It was too late to hitch back home, so we spent that night in an old feed bin surrounded by scrub piñon. Next morning we climbed out and faced a man and four kids with two sets of clothes between them. The man let his shovel sag when he got a look at us. Didn't mean to scare you, girls, he said, but I'm not having anyone else lay claim to these piñons before the nuts come due.

They escorted us to the road and said good-bye. They'll be waiting five months for those piñons, my sister said. They might as well lie down and die right now, if that's all they have in them to do.

We made it home before dark, but two days later we were back on the road, this time in a borrowed Ford. Let me drive, my sister said as we swerved along, but our mother only shook her head and cried all the way to Pie Town. When we pulled up to Aunt Honey's dugout, my aunt's husband burst out the front door as if he'd been waiting for us. Why'd you have those goddamn fancy flowers anyways? he shouted, and smacked his fist on the car.

My mother made a sound in her throat when she saw Aunt Honey. Stay put, she said to us. She got out of the car and held up her hands to ward off the husband. We didn't know, my mother said, we didn't know they were poison, how could we have known? She put her arms around Aunt Honey, and they disappeared into the house.

My aunt's husband shouted at us, and his chin shook. Where the hell am I supposed to get wood enough for a coffin to bury my boy? Goddamn you all to hell. Then he turned and staggered away across the pasture, and sometimes he tripped from stepping in gopher holes.

Who'd have thought they'd be fool enough to eat our tulips, my sister said. It is strange, but this is the moment of my life that I come back to most. I felt her harsh words like a blow. After that day her tenderness was gone.

That is what I have always grieved from that day, and not the death of a young boy. I am ashamed of that.

But at Mesa Portales on those birthdays, my sister would be easier. We'd stand together with the wind pressing our skirts up against us and look toward Pie Town as if we could spot it from the shine off a tin roof or two. From higher up and far away, our lives didn't overcome us so much, and we could talk about them without hardness. I believe this had to do with the air and the light with the view all around us.

Also I have been with Lorna up at Mesa Portales many times. To be up there is like church, but better. It is full of joys and sorrows, and the only answer is to live with them.

These are things in my life, and you built a house right over them. That is why I have never been to see it. You didn't know it was wrong, but I can't help how I feel about it. I have judged you for this, but also I have forgiven you, and you won't like either part of that.

You are a great joy to me, Agatha. But if I go up there and stand inside your house, I am afraid that I won't see Pie Town anymore. I am not like you, I can't give everything up and move on to the next place. I don't like to forget the bad things. I don't want to.

I'll put this letter with the others instead of leaving it somewhere to surprise you as we do. When you find it unopened in the drawer, then you will wonder why and approach it in a different frame of mind. This is a love letter no different in its way from all the others. But it may take you some time to see it.

From your Alice

6

PLANT SAGE AND WILD OREGANO on Alice and Lorna's grave in an effort to disguise it. I wash my hands. I tell myself I can move forward, as I have always done.

But something has gone wrong with the ocean canyon. There is no movement in the rock, no wind or cloud shadows. It is still as death, a faded paper cutout. But I can hear, in the occasional tremble of air across the valley, a kind of whispering. When I listen I understand that it is Ma Binney and the widows, singing as they did all those years ago at the pickers' camp in deepest evening, when something came over them and their voices were like the angels'. I was young when I knew them, when I left them all behind without a second thought; but even though I turn away from the ocean canyon and cover my ears, still I hear them singing to me, as if I were one of their own.

I stare at the grave. Alice once explained to me that she had been a churchgoer her whole life. She liked the singing and the little children and the socializing and the potluck after Sunday service. But she didn't believe in heaven or hell. All the family try to comfort me by saying that when I die Lorna will come to take me to our everlasting home, she said. But in my bones I don't believe that. I never have.

On the ledge at dusk I feel the back of my neck prickle and turn to find a mountain lion not far behind me, its tail twitching. It is not an easy procedure to get to my feet. Haw! I shout, and hold my hands over my head to be as large as possible. The mountain lion continues twitching its tail, and I feel the ocean canyon at my back, the long drop down to its rock floor. I think of my invincibility, which I have never doubted. I close my eyes. When I open them again the mountain lion is gone, but I find its scat at the edge of the mesa.

These are difficult moments, and when I see dim shapes dart in the corner of my eye I am afraid it is Julien come to confuse me, because difficult moments are what he likes best. But I don't hear his voice or feel him near. It is some consolation to me that perhaps this means he may never come again.

The visitor who does come is Alice herself. She appears in my kitchen when I am making a peanut butter and tomato sandwich. She is laughing. I have never heard this kind of laughing from Alice before, a kind of taunting. She is pointing at my sandwich as if it is ridiculous. Has she considered how ridiculous she herself now is, toppled into a grave with her daughter, the both of them?

But as soon as I have this thought I put an end to it. Alice is the one at the short end of the stick, after all. It's not her fault her life has ended. In some moments I forget that there is nothing to her now, and I allow myself to wonder: In death has her rage at last burst forth? It was never credible to me that she didn't have any. When I first knew her I imagined she papered it over, lulled it with pots of flowers and graveside chats and iced tea with cookies.

But if a person has all eternity to ponder, if the hands of a neon clock no longer mark down the moments of her life because she no longer has one, if all she has is to look backward because there is no life to live forward, well, what would she feel?

7

VERONICA APPEARS AT MESA PORTALES. Her eyes are full of a beautiful, stern light because she has come to accuse me. I have never been so glad to see her.

I didn't ask you to come, I say.

We need to talk. She pauses for effect.

For an instant I wonder if she somehow knows about Alice, buried by my own hand not twenty feet from us. But the set of her features is entirely self-interested, and so I know why she has come. It has to do with my advice to Dan. Well, I don't want to argue about that. I make sure to speak before she says another word.

Alice is dead, I say.

It makes me feel alive, to stop someone before they cross me. And it does stop her. All the righteousness drains out of her. It suits her better, non-righteousness does. Her blush of shame and dismay is a gorgeous shade of pink.

Oh no, oh, Agatha, Veronica says.

She steps forward and puts her arms around me. I don't protest. I am relieved to have said it out loud: that Alice is dead.

Yes, I say. In fact she's very dead.

Veronica disentangles herself. She's very dead?

I know what Veronica is thinking. I'm a precise person. As regards most things, I don't believe in extra when extra isn't needed. Dead is dead. There's no need for very dead. Veronica is wondering if I've decided that Alice is simply dead to me. Perhaps I am announcing this so Veronica will know that Alice has gone the way of the dean of the College of Fine Arts, also the rude man who runs the grocery in Jemez Springs, and most of the minimalists. Georgia was on my list a couple years ago, but I brought her back by casually pronouncing her name in conversation after an extended expulsion. *Georgia has a recipe for rye bread that Alice tried the other day; it was not bad.*

Alice died, I say definitively.

Veronica softens again. Agatha, when?

Well, the other day.

After you dropped me off?

I shake my head.

Earlier than that? She gapes at me.

I don't answer.

Wait, she says. Before we went to Taos?

I feel a new sensation: that I am shrinking while Veronica is growing. I sit down heavily on my stool.

She moves forward as if to touch me, but I hold up my hand to ward her off. She sits down on the ground next to me instead.

You're scaring me, she says. Tell me what's happening.

Alice is dead, I say. I found her in her backyard. Just a few days ago. A heart attack or stroke, I don't know what.

My voice catches, and I cough to cover it. I press my lips together.

Agatha, Veronica says, does anyone else know that Alice died?

Now you do, I say.

She takes that in. I feel how my words are a burden to her.

Has there been a funeral?

Not the usual sort, I say.

Now she is on high alert. She stands up and begins pacing back and forth near the ledge. Then she turns on her heel and walks over to the grave. She stands right on top of it and stares down, considering. Then she takes a large step back.

Agatha, she says. Her voice is firm, as if she is now coming to the point of things.

I nod and gesture toward the grave to indicate that her idea is correct.

Oh my God, she says, and claps a hand over her mouth.

She was never fond of you, I say.

At this Veronica stares at me and laughs wildly, in fact hysterically. Stop, Agatha, she says. Just stop.

Before I can respond, the high wail of a baby splits the air. It is a sound that anyone would agree is worse than the noise the cat makes when it clings to Alice's screen door.

We both turn our heads toward the sound. Veronica rushes to the car. I follow her and peer in through the rolled-down windows. Inside is a baby. This baby is hot and irritated, with powerful lungs. I spot a rash on its leg near the diaper. It has bright orange hair that sticks out in all directions, and its eyes are dark hazel ringed with gold, like Dan's.

Veronica opens the door and murmurs, picks it up and turns to me.

For God's sake, I say. This is no place for a baby.

Also I hear Alice's voice as if she were right beside me. What a beautiful baby! What a beautiful baby! and so on.

This is no place for a baby! I shout it this time.

Veronica's face flushes deep red. That's what you're worried about right now?

The baby scrunches its eyes and wails against the sun.

Get it into the shade, I say, and point toward the house.

She doesn't move. Explain it to me, she says. What is going on? Explain it.

Babies are not for people like me, I say. I didn't think they were for people like you either.

That's not what I'm asking you to explain, Agatha!

Veronica is the one shouting now, jabbing her finger toward the grave. Her shouting upsets the baby, it waves its tiny starfish hands in alarm and howls. She jiggles it up and down, as if that would be the least bit calming to anyone.

You can't possibly succeed with a baby, I say.

She takes a deep breath as if to calm herself. I'm not an artist like you, she says.

It doesn't matter what you are, I say, if you are also a mother. I am older than you and I know better.

You don't! Now she is shouting. You don't know as much as you think you do, Agatha.

I know precisely how much I know, I say, and it is an immense amount with enormous range.

But Veronica continues as if I haven't said a word. And I know what else you did, I know you told Dan to take Margot away from me. To get a lawyer! I'll never let that happen. How could you do that to me?

Give it to me, I say, and hold out my hands. Give me your baby.

Neither of us moves—until abruptly she does, she steps forward and puts the baby in my hands. As if, had she thought about it for one second longer, she never would.

Frankly I'm surprised at this surrender. Also I don't know what to do with this baby. It has stopped crying. It feels very delicate, very trustful in my hands. It lifts its eyes to me and it is not afraid.

But Veronica is afraid. Fear and panic are all over her face. She makes a small sound. She wrings her hands and steps toward me.

I tuck the baby into the crook of my elbow and put one hand gently on top of its head. I look at Veronica severely.

What do you think? I say. Do you think I'll hurt your baby?

As soon as these words come out my mouth I realize that I can't allow a split second for her to waver in her answer. It will be the death of us.

I turn away from her and face the ocean canyon. I gather the baby up tighter in my arms and say to it, Hush immediately. And I sing a lullaby from the dim glimmer of my own childhood. Who sung it to me I can't recall. Maybe I heard it sung to someone else.

My Bonnie lies over the ocean,
My Bonnie lies over the sea.
My Bonnie lies over the ocean,
Oh, bring back my Bonnie to me.

Bring back, bring back,
Oh, bring back my Bonnie to me.

When I finish there is a space of perfect quiet. In it I think of Alice.

Veronica holds out her arms and I put the baby back in them.

I feel different, peeled.

What a beautiful baby, I say.

Veronica clears her throat. Why did you tell Dan to take Margot away from me?

I frown, because why would she bring that up again?

Dan may have misunderstood, I say.

Veronica waits.

Or perhaps I was wrong. I manage to say this grandly, as if I am bestowing her a favor, one that it is not necessary for me to grant.

You were wrong, she says.

And she leaves it there because Veronica is not a rigid or unforgiving person, and anyway, there is no one else like me.

8

WITH VERONICA AT MESA PORTALES, the day has softened. The wind is pushing dark clouds closer, but the ocean canyon has come back to life, it shifts and shimmers. It is not unusual to be stunned into silence at Mesa Portales, but today it is not only the ocean canyon that provokes our quiet; today we also feel Alice's grave at our backs.

Veronica nurses the baby, too often, every time it makes a peep.

You're making a bad habit, I say. It will think you're at its beck and call.

She's a baby, Veronica says. I am at her beck and call.

You may be sorry later.

She pretends not to hear me. I hope she doesn't let her pride get in the way of taking advice. Just because she opposed what I thought in regard to having the baby doesn't mean that she should therefore discount all advice I might offer in the future. She can't think straight with the baby around, that much is clear.

Veronica puts a hand on my shoulder. Her other hand is on the baby, and I feel a warm jolt at the line of touch between the three of us. I sit very still until my breath steadies, and then I relax just a little.

When the baby falls asleep, Veronica carries her into the house and puts her down on the bed. I hear the determined crunch of her footsteps coming back to the ledge.

She sits down and looks at me with a gentle expression on her face, an expression I have not seen from her before. In fact it may be a kind of love.

I believe you, she says. I believe you about how Alice died.

Well, why wouldn't you? I say.

I'm not sure everyone else will believe you, though, she says, considering that you buried her up here without telling anyone.

You were in shock, she says. Maybe you still are.

I know you loved her, she says.

We have to fix this, she says. I have to figure out how.

Because it's the kind of mistake that might land you in jail, she says, if people don't understand.

One more thing, I say, and gesture toward the grave. Lorna is there with her.

I watch Veronica struggle through a brief confusion before becoming entirely alarmed.

Agatha, no, she wails.

I lift my face to the breeze, which is dry and gentle, with the scent of a thunderstorm coming. It is a relief to tell Veronica. Perhaps it means I trust her.

Didn't you say that man with the chickens is a lawyer? she says. Maybe we can ask him for advice.

At that I laugh and get up off my stool. I'll make sandwiches, I say.

Check on Margot, please? she asks distractedly.

But I won't, because anyone knows to let sleeping babies lie.

The front door is ajar. Even before I step inside I sense something or someone who isn't a baby. My ears are very good, and alongside the hum of bugs and the low rush of wind, I hear a rustle from the bedroom.

9

I EDGE SILENTLY TOWARD THE BED, making sure to stay just beyond the circle of light from the lantern on the table. I imagine an animal, a mountain lion or coyote. My brain refuses thoughts of Margot, the terrible possibilities, her tiny body on the bed.

What I find is Josey, bent over Margot and making soothing noises. When he sees me he leaps forward and wraps his arms all the way around my middle.

I open my mouth to say, What in hell are you doing sneaking around here, Josey? But he reaches up and presses a hand over my mouth. This upsets me terribly, so I jerk my head away and grab his wrists together in my own big hand. He is covered in a layer of dirt, his hair sticking out in all directions, his face swollen.

Josey, I say, what is going on?

Before he can answer, Frank Jr. steps inside my house, as if he has been lurking around just outside to trap me.

I let go of Josey's wrists. He grabs my shirtsleeve.

Stop it, Josey, I say. We're not afraid of Frank Jr.

Frank Jr.'s boots and jeans are also covered in a crust of dirt; his face is smudged and on one arm is a long scratch. He wipes his mouth.

Messing with a man's truck is against the law, he says. I caught Josey red-handed. That little delinquent will go to juvie for this.

Josey has a black eye, I say.

Bruises on my arms too. Josey sounds more like himself, no longer afraid.

I scowl at Frank Jr. How'd you get here if he damaged your truck like you're claiming.

It died on us about six miles back, he says. We walked the rest of the way.

Most likely you hadn't been maintaining it properly.

Shut up, Agatha! He grips the table as if restraining himself. No doubt in my mind that you put him up to it. I brought him with me to show you I know your game. I know you're hiding Ma. There's nowhere else she'd be.

Your mother is at the place in Taos, I say, as you well know.

Frank Jr. slams his hand down on the table. Listen, I went to Taos! The woman there said Ma was sleeping and there were settling-in rules. That I should come back in one month. The truth is at first I believed her because I wanted to. I knew Ma would cry and want to go home, and I didn't want to feel bad. So I left. But then I got to thinking. It didn't feel right, like something fishy was going on. Then I catch Josey sneaking around, and I know, Agatha, I *know*.

I told you Mrs. Alice isn't here! Josey says. But he casts a sidelong glance at me to be sure.

There is a bright flash of lightning followed quickly by a boom of thunder. The baby starts crying, a whimpering that rises up to a wail, and Josey ducks back toward the bed.

You got a baby here too? Frank Jr. is incredulous.

As far as I know Frank Jr. is unpleasant only to grown women, but there's no reason to take any chances. It's the cat, I say. The place in Taos wouldn't let your mother have it there.

All at once the rain arrives and hammers the roof in a concussion of sound, the kind of storm that arrives in deep summer and washes out roads, occasionally drowns a person or two in an arroyo.

Veronica rushes in out of the rain and stops short, startled by the sight of us. The cries rachet up, and now it's undeniable that there's an actual baby in my house. Veronica bolts past us to the bedroom.

Frank Jr. and I glower at each other while she murmurs to Margot.

Who's that? Frank Jr. asks.

A friend of mine.

Who else you got up here?

That's all.

He snorts. Get Ma for me, I'm tired of waiting. I know she's here. God knows what you've done to make her like you so much, Agatha. You're a bad influence, you've turned Josey here into a criminal!

Veronica appears in the doorway, holding Margot. She throws Frank Jr. a disgusted glance. Who are you? she says. You're loud and you're scaring my baby.

It's laughable how he clears his throat and says, in a gentle manner, Why, I'm Frank.

This is Alice's son, I say.

Veronica's face clouds.

Where's my mother? he asks her.

She hesitates. I haven't seen your mother here.

Veronica has not strictly told a lie, but her words have the ring of a crooked truth. Frank Jr. eyes her suspiciously.

You can't show up here shouting accusations and causing trouble, I say to distract him. You need to go.

I'm not going without Ma, he says.

I look over at Veronica. Take Josey and the baby outside, I say. Go on!

She grips Margot with one arm and takes Josey by the hand, pulls him toward the door. He looks back at me, but I nod firmly.

Once they're gone, I turn to Frank Jr.

You can't give a child a black eye and drag him by the wrist for miles, I say. You're not the law around here. I heard what happened to your father, but that's no way to go about things.

He is taken by surprise. My pops deserved what he got. You act like you're the only one who cares about Ma. Do you think I won't miss her when she's in Taos, is that what you think? I've been missing her a long time already. She's not how she was.

A vision of him as a young boy comes to me, Alice covering him in kisses. I am carrying inside me the fact of Alice being dead, the terribleness of that, and I don't want to carry that terribleness for him as well. I try to squelch this sympathy; I shake my head to clear it.

When Pops passed I wasn't sorry, he says. I figured, I've got my own life now out from under him, I'll do what I like, why shouldn't Ma? But I don't like *you*, Agatha, that's the pure fact of it. You aren't the person I had in mind as a friend to her and you know what I mean. This dump up here doesn't belong to you, it belongs to *me*. Ma is going to live in a decent place where she'll be taken care of, and you're going to go on back to wherever you came from.

He grabs my flashlight off the hook next to the door and heads outside.

Ma! he shouts. I stand in the doorway and watch as he hunches down against the rain, shining the flashlight around as he walks. The light wavers briefly on Veronica sitting in her car holding the baby, Josey in the passenger seat beside her. They both flinch when the beam hits their faces, and I see Josey reach across Veronica to lock the door closest to Frank Jr.

But Frank Jr. strides right past the car and then straight across the grave without any intuitions arising in his chest whatsoever. He stomps off into the wet dark toward the mesa's far end, as if we've hidden Alice in the outhouse.

I shout to Veronica and Josey to come into the house. Veronica glances back at me, then shakes her head at Josey. I lumber over to her car and slide into the back seat.

Inside is a change of atmosphere. The rain is loud but muffled, and I can smell the tangy sweat of Veronica, the familiar ripeness of Josey, the milky smell of Margot.

That young man has a number of problems, I say. Come back inside and we'll stay out of his way until he cools down.

We need to leave, Veronica says, and starts the engine. It's not safe for Margot or for any of us.

It's not safe to leave, I say loudly, to make my voice heard over the rain on the car roof. We'll be lucky if the road's not washed out already.

It's true that the road washes out now and then, and that it can be dangerous in heavy weather. But I don't care about the road. What I won't do is leave Frank Jr. alone at Mesa Portales to do his worst.

Come back in the house, I say. I get out and slam the door behind me. Hurry up!

But Veronica hands Josey the baby, leans over, and locks the door I just got out of. Then she starts the car! I bang on the passenger-side window to stop her, and she ignores me. But she has miscalculated as regards certain loyalties, because Josey handles the situation by getting out of the car with the baby and running back toward the house. I follow. Veronica shouts after us, but Josey keeps going until he's inside the house, and it only takes an instant after the baby starts crying that Veronica is inside with us too.

At least Josey has good sense, I say.

Now that Veronica is back inside my house, she has lost the will for a fight with me over leaving. Josey hands her the baby, and she directs him to drag the table over to block the door. I open my mouth to protest, to point out once again that we're not afraid of Frank Jr. But I reconsider, because the truth is that I'm tired. I don't want him bursting in to bother us.

Frank Jr. tries the door, then shines the flashlight in the window. I'm not leaving, he shouts, and I won't be sleeping in the meantime, so don't try sneaking Ma out from wherever you've got her!

He disappears from sight. When I peer out the window, I see him settled down by the front door, leaning back against the house.

I don't like any part of him touching my house. I don't like it at all. Also it bothers me how he lets the rain run down his face without wiping it away. It's not natural to sit in pouring rain without trying to get out from under it.

Veronica announces that she will be taking the bed for the night, as it's not safe for Margot to sleep on the floor.

Nobody is going to step on the baby by accident, I say. Anyway, it's my bed.

You're welcome to share it with us, she says.

No bed is big enough for that, I say crossly.

Agatha, Josey says, and tugs on my sleeve. He has organized a mattress for me out of pillows and extra blankets. He has squared all the edges and lined it up perfectly with the north and west walls. I admire his work.

Thank you, Josey, I say. That's very considerate. I look at Veronica when I say this.

I pull the chair over to the impromptu mattress, because the chair is a necessary interval. I sit down and take off my shoes, lift the purse strap off and over my shoulders. I ease myself onto the floor and use the purse as a pillow for my head; the letters crackle quietly under my cheek.

Turn the lantern out, Josey.

None of us make any small talk, as if we are determined to fall asleep and arrive at morning as soon as possible. I think of Frank Jr. just outside the door. I am suffocated by all these people, their breathing and the things they want. It is not like my house at all.

10

A T DAWN FRANK JR. POUNDS on the door. Veronica bolts upright on the bed. Josey rubs his eyes and removes his foot from my side, and Margot starts wailing. I won't stay in this madhouse another minute.

Stay put, I say to Josey and Veronica. I pull my purse on and push the table away from the door.

The door flies open and Frank Jr. almost falls into the room. Behind him the ground is steaming in the sun after such a rain, and the fresh air is wonderful.

Frank Jr.'s eyes are wild and his fist is raised for more pounding, but when he sees me he takes a step back. I woke up and went to take a leak, he says. I saw your poor excuse for a garden and thought, Why not piss on it? and while I was pissing I got to noticing. Strange shape for a garden; strange location for one too. Strange how the earth is sunk just there. Then I know what I'm standing on!

I look past him and right away see how the rain has revealed the grave, which now sags a few inches down into itself. The sage and oregano have been yanked up and tossed away, and there is an area of pronounced digging at one end. My shovel lies on the ground nearby.

I know that sheet! he shouts.

I step outside to face him. I pull the door shut behind me and fold my arms across my chest.

He lunges forward and punches me in the face. I let out a cry, I stagger but don't fall. I may be old but I'm not weak. I'm not a pushover. I am in fact quite solid. Also I have suffered punches before so I am unsurprised by the feel of it.

Does it make you feel better to hit an old woman? I ask, and before he can answer I punch him right back. He ducks, but even so I land a good blow on the top of his head.

He straightens back up, dazed, and starts crying, an angry, desperate heaving. The quality of this crying seems to be brought on by something deeper than my punch and shows no signs of stopping. The sound of it is terrible. Usually I am resolute in what I do and don't believe in second thoughts, but an unfamiliar impulse comes over me now, and it is the impulse to apologize.

The door behind me swings open, and Veronica steps out. Josey also comes outside, holding Margot, and stands next to me.

Frank Jr. ignores them and leans toward me, wipes the tears off his face with his open palm. His face is haggard, as if all his life he has expected the worst and here it is. Do you know what it's like, Agatha? Digging up your own mother.

Josey makes a pained noise. Mrs. Alice is dead?

I don't answer Frank Jr., because obviously it's terrible to dig someone up. I've dug up two people recently and I don't wish it on anyone.

Instead I take Josey's hand and squeeze it gently. She is dead, I say quietly.

Why'd you kill her, Agatha? Frank Jr. says.

He's asking a sincere question, I can hear it. Mostly I don't care what people think of me. But I wouldn't want anyone to believe me capable of hurting Alice.

Frank Jr., I say, we don't like each other, but listen to what I am saying to you. I never killed your mother, I never would and don't ever think it of me. I'd hurt myself or anyone else before I'd ever hurt her. That's the truth. I found her in the garden. She passed alone, sitting right next to Lorna.

His tears dry up in a rush of anger. A likely story, and what's your proof? he demands.

Veronica clears her throat. I was there too, she says. Your mother was in her backyard when we arrived, sitting next to Lorna's grave. She was peaceful, she had a smile on her face, but she had passed.

Frank Jr. is incredulous. And you agreed with Agatha that it was right to bury her here and not tell anyone?

Veronica hesitates, because that is a bridge too far for her.

I didn't know that part of it, she says, glancing sideways at me. I assumed everything would proceed as these things usually do. But I promise you, your mother died a natural death. I saw her. I'm sorry for your loss.

I surprise myself by touching Frank Jr.'s arm. You are having an awful shock and I can't blame you for it. I loved your mother too. But also be sensible in this moment. There was no wrongdoing.

No wrongdoing? Frank Jr. knocks my hand off his arm. Are you joking? He backs away from us and then paces back and forth, waves his arms around, and shakes a fist at me. I didn't like it, but I figured what was the harm, I didn't want Ma to be lonely. What a mistake that was, to have you hanging around!

He stops pacing at the very lip of the ledge. Just a step beyond him, the emptiness of the ocean canyon waits.

Veronica catches my eye and nods, a warning and a reassurance both. Then she walks over to Frank Jr. and puts a hand firmly on his shoulder as if to comfort him.

That's enough now, she says. I know it's hard and it's a disgrace the way Agatha handled it. But your mother died all on her own. I'll swear it on a Bible or on my baby, in court or anywhere else I need to. And it's the truth. Everyone will believe me. Do you?

The ocean canyon flickers to life. I hold my breath, because I know Veronica. She is willing to push him if he answers wrong, and this is how it would go: Frank Jr. falling into the ocean canyon, at first his arms and legs frozen wide in surprise, and after that would begin a frantic flailing.

Instead Frank Jr. looks her in the eye. I do believe you, he says unhappily. I don't want to, but I do. But she goes and buries Ma up here! It's wrong, it's disgusting! She needs to pay for what she's done.

I agree with you, Veronica says sympathetically. She inches closer to him, her hand still on his shoulder.

So you're a Judas now! I say to her.

Shut up for one minute, Agatha, she says.

Pull yourself together, Veronica! I say. Frank Jr. is a bad person who was not kind to his mother.

That's a lie, Frank Jr. says.

Like father, like son. I scowl at him.

I'm not like him, he says.

Just because a person believes themself to be good does not make that belief correct, I say.

He laughs meanly, as if I've told a clever joke against myself.

Frank Jr.! Veronica says sharply, squeezes his shoulder to get his attention.

She has coiled forward almost imperceptibly, her calves flexed and a taut anticipation in the angle of her arm.

He looks over at her, their faces only inches apart.

How much do you want? she asks him.

For a minute we all stare at her, confused. Even Margot turns her head.

Then Frank Jr.'s eyes light up.

I want all of it, he says. I want everything she's got.

Veronica smiles and takes her hand off his shoulder.

THREE

S OMEONE IS CALLING ME: ALCIE, Alcie! Coffee!

It doesn't suit me, that name. Alcie is a bit of birdsong, light and sweet. Not like Agatha, which is low and tight in the jaw.

Well, I do want coffee. Even before I open my eyes, I can feel that the light in the room is different, that the storm has passed. Out the window I see snow on the mountains. Alice's suitcase, now covered in a thin lick of dust, is tucked neatly under the bed where I left it those few months ago. I have also been left undisturbed since arriving here. Everyone is busy with naps and soft food and asking when their daughters might take them away for a visit. Mostly they haven't thought of me at all.

I button my shirt and put on my overalls, go out into the hallway. Through the window the dogwood's branches are draped in white.

The coffee here is terrible, but I'll drink it one more time.

When I parked my pickup out front two days ago, Francesca stood on the porch with her arms crossed, watching me. I adjusted the purse across my chest, picked up the chicken-lawyer's clock from the passenger seat, and got out of the pickup.

In a chair next to Francesca was the old man, wearing a wool hat and with a blanket across his lap for the cold. He peered eagerly and lifted a hand when he saw me, no doubt in hopes of seeing Veronica, and struggled halfway up before sitting heavily back down. Francesca put out her arm for him to take hold of, and this time he hauled himself up to standing.

She steadied him and narrowed her eyes at me. Where are your belongings? she called. You can't show up with your purse and a clock and nothing else. This is not the Hotel La Fonda.

I'm not bringing anything else, I said.

She frowned. I don't think you are Alcie Johnson. I've heard some things.

But still you have received your money, I pointed out.

I don't want money for an empty room, she said. It's wasteful. Someone else would like to have it, with its two windows.

I'm only staying until the weather clears, I said. After that I'll have the payments stopped, and you can do what you want with the room.

Francesca considered, then held the door open for me.

This time when I walked down the hallway I stared at the dirty handprints with a dangerous hope in my chest. *Alcie Johnson.* I had a wild stray wish, a tender shoot: that Alice was alive, that I would open the door to her room and there she would be. But I knew that she would not.

Yet inside the room I felt improved. I was seized with the feeling that a wonderful prank had been played by me: I had done it, here I was, hidden away. The light inside the room was tinged with a creamy pink, and there was a great sense of spaciousness. I felt a bit of regret, as I could see that in fact this room was a place where a person could live.

I lay down on the bed and played possum to calm myself. No one would look for me here, no one would find me, not before I was already gone.

Later I propped the chicken-lawyer's clock up on the bureau and plugged it in. Its lights flickered on-off, on-off, and then it began its hum of neon red and green. Josey had brought it as a present for me, on his final visit to Mesa Portales. Why, Josey! I'd said. You know how much I've always hated this clock. How did you know it was exactly the present for me? We laughed as we looked out over the ocean canyon, imagining the chicken-lawyer discovering that his clock had vanished. There is nobody who understands me in the way that Josey does.

I eased the suitcase out from under the bed and took out Lorna's brooch, still tucked inside Alice's slipper. I balanced the brooch on my knee and considered it. The blue stone, the tarnished silver, the careful beak of the thunderbird, its deftly sketched wings. Perhaps I could understand something from it about Alice, about Lorna—perhaps even about me, Agatha. Blue stone, tarnished silver, careful beak, deft wings. But though I tried to look long enough to see beyond the brooch itself, its meaning eluded me.

It did not work in the same way of my paintings, but this was not the fault of the thunderbird. Lately I had come to understand that the only vision I had was my own and I could not see beyond it. All my life I had believed this to be my greatest strength. But it is humbling to live in this world.

EVERYONE HAD COME TO MESA Portales for Alice's funeral, the whole town.

I told Veronica to buy cookies, but only my favorite kind, and she did this, she bought sixteen packages of marshmallow puffs, each puff covered in a thin chocolate shell and nestled in crinkly plastic. Veronica arranged the packages in perfect rows, four by four, on the table in my kitchen. I should've got paper napkins, she said. And cups!

I took a few cookies immediately and sat in my chair while Veronica scurried around, sweeping and dusting and fretting over the state of the outhouse at the far end of the mesa. I licked the chocolate off my fingers, then wiped my fingers on my overalls. I only laughed when Veronica said, Agatha, quit acting like a child and help get ready. Margot looked over at me, and she laughed too.

But when Veronica went outside and started fussing over Alice's grave, I got up from my chair. Stop immediately, I said.

She had a shovel in her hand and slapped at the dirt with the flat of it. It's not tidy! she said. It doesn't look respectful. She looked at me meaningfully. We can't give anyone an excuse to redo the grave, Agatha.

Veronica had offered Frank Jr. triple the Bureau of Land Management offer for Mesa Portales, and he took it without bargaining further. He had no vision, no imagination, and never dreamed that triple the price would not ruin me. When Veronica offered an additional small amount for Alice's house—so Lorna can stay where she is, Veronica said—he accepted that too, grinning as if he couldn't believe our foolishness.

I did not agree with any of this, as no price can be put on Mesa Portales. Also I did not want to own it. I only wanted to live on it. But in that moment I was overcome with a heavy misery, and it silenced me. While they dickered, I stared at my hands with concern because I did not know where to put them. They hung at my sides and twitched in distress as if they belonged to someone else entirely. This deal that Veronica and Frank were making on my behalf seemed an obscure strike against Mesa Portales, as if it were now somehow tainted.

Just beyond us was the grave, a hasty scattering of dug-up earth. I could see the flowered sheet, it was no longer blue, it was dirty gray with spots of ocher. Josey chirruped to Margot and moved closer to me.

But what about Ma? Frank Jr. said, as if suddenly recalling an inconvenient fact. I guess we'll move her down to the cemetery.

I was jolted out of my suffering. No, I said. Alice stays here or there is no deal.

You're the one who needs this deal, Frank Jr. sneered. You buried my mother without my permission. You didn't even tell me she was dead!

Digging your mother back up will change nothing, Veronica said to him soothingly. It will only cause trouble.

She glanced over at me with a tremor of worry on her face. I knew that she was thinking of Lorna.

Agatha is offering more money than you will ever get again, Veronica said. If you move your mother, you will have all the trouble and scandal of it and not enough money to do as you like in your life. You'd be cutting off your own nose.

Frank Jr. pretended to consider but very soon nodded his head in agreement. He had shrunk slightly with the shame of this bargain, and that was a consolation to me, also invigorating; it is good to have an enemy, as it is clarifying and gives purpose.

Veronica tore a page from her notebook and wrote down the terms in her tidy handwriting. Then she pointed her pen at Frank Jr. There will be no double-crossing or going back on this deal, she said. Alice died of natural causes, and her wish to be buried quietly on Mesa Portales is being honored. You are selling Mesa Portales and your mother's house to Agatha. That is the only story I will tell in any circumstance. I am a witness to this deal and so is Josey.

Leave Josey out of it, I said.

Veronica shrugged in unconcerned agreement. Everyone will believe me anyway, she said.

The sun was behind Veronica when she said these words and it cast a powerful glow around her, as if she had a kind of celestial authority. It's true anyone would believe her over the likes of me or Frank Jr. A young mother with a child has power in this world in certain situations, and this would be one of them.

Frank Jr. signed his name, using my stool as a table. Then Veronica put the pen in my hand. Go on, Agatha, she said.

The weather at that moment was very fine: the bright sun, the clear air of morning with no hint of the heat to come. I thought of Alice, how I had never held her hand up here in this light. I thought of Pie Town, which I could never see. I thought of Alice and her sister, looking out over the ocean canyon as the wind pressed up against their skirts. I looked at my house and Alice's grave just beyond it, and I thought of all the things that I had done.

I touched my purse of letters. I did not wish to become the owner of Mesa Portales. But I signed to make Frank Jr. go away, because this time I would move forward in order to turn one thing back. That thing was my house, and I would do it for Alice.

It was a strange feeling: doing what I did not want to do. As soon as I had signed, the ocean canyon retreated slightly from me, I felt it like a chill in my bones.

Veronica slipped the paper back into her notebook and announced that we would contact my shark-lawyer for the payment and that Frank Jr. should advise his chicken-lawyer about a contract and the deed. Then Veronica took him by the arm and walked him over to her car. She handed him her keys. Once he was in the car, she leaned down and spoke to him in a low tone before he drove away.

I didn't care for a private conversation between Veronica and Frank Jr. What did you say to him? I demanded.

That I'll kill him if he tells anyone you buried Alice up here without asking. I made sure to smile at him when I said it. She flashed her teeth to demonstrate.

Her smile gave me pause and I believed her entirely. I felt a new respect for her, or possibly a kind of caution, at how far she was willing to go in matters that pertain to me. In the end it's true she has been a person I can count on, and I did not predict that.

You still have enough money left to do whatever you want, she said, and you can sell more work. Also we can write and sell the biography. She laughed. Though of course now it can't be a tell-all.

She looked at Josey, who gently jiggled Margot up and down to calm her. Josey, this day is a secret we take to our graves, can you make me that promise?

Josey nodded his head but with a large measure of disgust, because he would never say a word about anything secret or important regarding me.

AND SO WE CAME TO the morning of the funeral, when Veronica and I stood staring at Alice's untidy grave. The mound of it sloped crookedly and was scattered with clumps of dirt and rocks and twigs. After Frank Jr. drove away in Veronica's car, I hadn't wanted to see the flowered sheet for even one more minute, and I had hurriedly filled the grave back in. But it's true that the work was slipshod and not my usual way of doing things.

Give me the shovel, I said to Veronica.

I worked steadily all afternoon. I used my T square and level and also my compass, and in the end the mound was perfectly even and gently sloping, shaped to align with the ocean canyon and the setting sun. With my trowel and a cloth I roughed it over entirely, spritzed it with water, and let it dry in the afternoon heat. Then I used a fine sandpaper to smooth the mound. I did these things in the way and in the rhythm that is needed for all my work, when I am aware of everything at once, everything except time—or perhaps it is the abeyance of time, like a glimpse of death itself.

When I was done the grave rose softly up out of the ground, a few shades darker than the land around it. It will burnish and harden in the weather, and in certain moments of slanted light, it will appear to glow. Slowly the earth will absorb it and it will be as if it has never been. This is in fact what I would wish for myself.

When I put away my tools, I thought again about the further thing that I must do, and that was to take down the house on Mesa Portales. I did not want to make Alice suffer in its shadow.

When Veronica saw that I was finished with the grave, she came outside. It's wonderful, she said, it's beautiful. You did right by them.

I told her not to speak in platitudes, as it suggests that she is not a serious person.

She ignored my remark, only cocked her head and suggested arranging adobe bricks around the grave to mark it out. But any border whatsoever would be entirely wrong and I didn't waste my breath in reply.

We heard the first cars making their way up the Mesa Portales road, which was rough after the rain. Others would park below the mesa and come up on foot.

Go clean up, Veronica said to me, smoothing Margot's flyaway wisps of hair. I'll greet everyone.

But there was no need for a cleanup. No one with any sense would think so, as a cleanup is not the important thing in any moment and is only busywork. Poor Margot, with a childhood of cleanups ahead of her.

FRANK JR.'S BAND PLAYED TO get the funeral started, and in that way it was the funeral of his dreams. He kept to guitar and left the singing to the man who sells silver jewelry laid out on a strip of velvet in front of the post office, and altogether the music was an improvement over anything else I have heard from Frank Jr.

The people from town ate all the cookies and took turns drinking water from the barrel with my one cup. Many people brought wildflower bouquets, but when they saw the grave they understood that to place anything on its perfection would be wrong. Instead they ringed the mound with them. It was very late in summer, but still there was purple bee balm, scarlet penstemon, and copper blanket flower, also a small bunch of lavender tied with twine.

Frank Jr. gathered everyone around the grave but broke down crying before finishing a sentence, so what good was he to anyone? The chicken-lawyer stepped in, and it's true that a few of the words he spoke were about me, and he called me Alice's loyal friend.

At these words of his everyone turned their faces to look at me, standing in the doorway of my house. I could see and feel from their expressions that they felt kindly toward me, and I did not expect that. I found that I looked at and felt kindly toward them in return.

The postmistress brought a small bouquet of dried apples, each apple carved in the shape of a rose in varying stages of bloom, with sticks as stems and tied together with blue ribbon. I saw that she was deep inside herself with sadness, so deep it was difficult for her to peer out at me at all. She clutched at my arm and sobbed.

She showed me the apple-roses, and I thought her work was very fine and told her so. When she placed this bouquet on top of the grave, right where Alice's hands might have held them up to her face to smell and to exclaim over, right where no one else had dared lay a bloom—well, I did not stop her. I suspected that she and Alice had been better friends than I imagined. Perhaps it has been no accident that I have called her the postmistress. But I don't care to know.

She lit a cigarette and wiped her cheeks. You should have told me she was doing so poorly, she said. I would've pushed more. Now it's too late for them.

Soon I would find out exactly what she meant by these words, but in that moment I thought only that she was strange and fitful with grief. She turned away from me and I have not seen her since, as if without Alice there is no need to speak to each other, and also it would be too painful.

NOWHERE IN THIS FUNERAL WAS Alice. She lay buried before us but otherwise did not participate. This was the most terrible thing, this lack of her, and it would never change. I was now in a kind of prison and had been given a life sentence. This thought of mine was the stuff of a bad love song, and so when Frank Jr.'s singer stood near me to see the view out over the ocean canyon, I told him this thought as a gift, as he might have use of it in a refrain.

But he only gestured with his beer bottle out over the ocean canyon. What a glorious place to rest for all eternity, he said.

I did not appreciate that he answered in the cadence of a preacher, which I suspected he was not.

Did you know Alice? I asked sternly.

He shook his head. I'm here for Frank Jr. But we all have mothers. There is no other way to come into this world. You can't make a life without one.

He smiled as if he had said something profound. Perhaps he had. Or perhaps he had said something that is in fact the opposite of profound and simply empty of meaning. In the past I had strong opinions about this kind of thing; but now I have been shaken and find it difficult to know for sure.

EVERYONE HAD COME TO MESA Portales for Alice's funeral, everyone except Josey.

He isn't feeling well, his mother said. She leaned forward to kiss my cheek. She smelled of sun and sweat, and her breath was hot in my ear. And I noticed that his new shoes are muddy, she whispered. The shine is off them.

She left a blackberry buckle on the kitchen table and a bouquet of pink stock at the foot of Alice's grave. Frank Jr.'s singer spotted her and rushed across the mesa to take her hand and introduce himself. But Josey's mother was not impressed with him and left soon after without another word to anyone.

I stood at the edge of the mesa, my back to the ocean canyon, and watched as she picked her way carefully down the road. I spoke when she was too far away to hear me. I'm sorry, I said to her, and meant it. Maybe one day I would stand closer.

Frank Jr.'s singer had ambled up beside me. He looked over in surprise at my words and then held up a cookie, used his big white teeth to crack through its chocolate shell. We watched as Josey's mother stopped at her car, gathered her hair up into her hands and braided it into a long gleaming string down her back. What a gal, Frank Jr.'s singer said. Then she got into her car and drove away.

BY EVENING EVERYONE WAS GONE. Veronica and Margot were the last to leave.

Did you get those brakes fixed? I asked as she put Margot in the car.

Veronica turned her head away from Margot and grinned at me. This grin was too much, it was big with happiness at the concern in my question, and I had to look away.

Are you sure you don't want us to stay? Veronica asked.

I did not want anyone.

Then at dusk I saw headlights in the distance, and Dan drove his car up on top of the mesa. He got the chair from the house and put it next to my stool on the ledge.

I'm sorry I didn't come before, he said.

I didn't know all the ways he meant those words, but I didn't press him as it turned out there had been a person that I wanted after all.

Well, you missed the refreshments, I said.

That's all right, he said, and held up a brown sack.

Inside were sandwiches that were the work of Melinda and unlike anything ever before eaten at Mesa Portales. Meat, cheese, tomato and sliced green peppers, mustard and a thin layer of green leaf, each sandwich wrapped neatly in wax paper. Small packets of salt and pepper rattled at the bottom of the sack, and also there were two oranges and a small package of fudge.

I took the top slice of bread off my sandwich and added the salt and pepper but otherwise did not change a thing.

Melinda sends her condolences, he said.

I nodded, because I knew from eating this sandwich that she did, and I was glad of the dark so that Dan could not see on my face how much I appreciated it.

I'm sorry about Alice, he said. She was a nice lady.

Something about his words made me laugh and released a bit of the heaviness in my chest.

Yes, I said, she was a nice lady.

We ate our sandwiches and said small things; these were not important things, it was just important that we said them. The heat, the price of gas, the old oak struck last week by lightning near the Señorita Canyon road; how Josey has a rock with flinty ripples like a shell that he keeps in his pocket to have the idea of an ocean with him; also a marshmallow on a stick that Alice burned black for me over a campfire years ago, just the way I like them.

Veronica told me she was with you when you found Alice, he said. I'm glad you weren't alone.

It startled me to learn that Veronica had not told him the truth, that she created a secret between us and apart from Dan. I thought about telling him but then did not. Perhaps he doesn't have to carry all the secrets.

Veronica would like this fudge, I said instead. You should give her some.

Dan sighed. Things are more complicated now, he said, because of the baby.

Also he said, Veronica needs you.

He threw his orange peels into the ocean canyon for the magpies and the prairie dogs to find.

I can't stay long, he said. It is hard for me now, to get away. A lot of people count on me.

I felt all these people, they crowded loudly between us. I didn't like it. But I only said, All right.

Before he left, Dan asked about the house, because he was the person to do things regarding it. Any problems? he said.

No, I said, because the problem with the house was not one that Dan could fix.

FOR A FEW DAYS AFTER the funeral, I saw no one. Josey had always come when he wanted, nothing had ever stopped him, not even his mother could, and so I knew that he stayed away on purpose. This weighed on me. When I looked out over the ocean canyon, I no longer felt free. In fact I often found it difficult to breathe, and for the first time I could not tolerate long hours in the sun. In evenings when the light eased, I moved my stool to Alice and Lorna's grave. I looked away from the ocean canyon. I thought about how to take down my house. It was a fine house, built by me, and it would not be easy.

Soon Veronica reappeared at Mesa Portales. She brought Margot with her, and also five shirts and two pairs of overalls, new underwear and socks. She was brisk, like a nurse or parole officer, and with a new authority about her. She collected my old clothes into a ragbag she happened to have handy, as she had started clearing out the piles of things in Alice's house.

Her house belongs to you now, she said. You can't just leave everything there in such a mess.

I shrugged, because I could do as I wished.

Veronica asked, did I want anything of Alice's from the house?

I shook my head and buttoned up a new shirt, pulled the new overalls up over it. I liked the stiff scratch of fabric against my skin.

Afterward we had coffee while Margot wailed because Veronica stopped her from putting tiny scraps of paper in her mouth. I told Veronica that she should look in Alice's hall closet for a box with things that Lorna had liked as a child: a loom and some colored pencils, also picture cards with holes punched out to thread with yarn.

But Veronica said no, Margot was too small, she'd try to poke herself in the eye with the pencils or strangle herself with the yarn, and that wouldn't do.

Well, she could at least scribble on the walls, I said crossly. The light on the east wall of Alice's bedroom will be good for that. But poor Margot, because Veronica won't allow that either.

I told Veronica that she could have Alice's house, that she and Margot could live there if they had nowhere to go, or even if they simply wanted to.

She looked at me and lifted her chin. Why, Agatha?

She waited. We watched Margot play.

It would be nice, I said, to have you both near.

Veronica smiled. Thank you, Agatha, she said.

I SAID TO VERONICA, I will take down my house.

Why? she asked over and over. You built it with your own hands! You've done your most important work here! It's your home!

I tried first with a sledgehammer and next an axe, but the adobe yielded only slightly. The bricks were still young and strong; also there was the matter of the roof and the vigas, and I could not do it alone.

I arranged for Uncle Felix to come give me his opinion. He had been there at the beginning, after all, when he brought the brick forms; perhaps he knew a tool for taking it all down. Veronica crossed her arms in disapproval as he walked around the house and looked at everything. It is important that nothing remain, I told him. It is important that it is as if the house has never been.

He looked over at the grave. What about Mrs. Johnson?

Well, she'll stay here, I said.

The adobe is still good, he said, and patted an outside wall. Knocking it down and carting away the bricks will be difficult and not cheap either, not all the way out here. You can salvage the vigas and windows but not much else. It'd sure be easier to leave it.

At this Veronica looked hopeful, but I shook my head.

You'd need two, three people to do it over a week or so, he said. I don't want this job. But perhaps you have some friends who would help you, if you're not in a hurry.

Before Uncle Felix left, I asked him to remind Josey how beautiful the view from Mesa Portales can be when the aspens turn gold and crimson on the mountains. That time of year will be here soon, I said.

Uncle Felix nodded. I'll tell Josey you asked after him. Just before his pickup disappeared down the mesa and out of sight, he honked the horn and waved his hand out the window.

THIS VISIT FROM UNCLE FELIX gave Veronica a new idea, one that made her cheerful about taking down my house.

What we'll do, Veronica said, is announce that you're working on a project at Mesa Portales that will outshine all the others.

By *others* Veronica meant the land art people. When I pointed out that I have no interest in that kind of work, no desire to fiddle around like boys with buckets in the sandbox pretending to be big men, she informed me she'd already told Fitz this absurd fiction.

He called *Artforum* to drop the news, and it'll run an article with a photo of you at Mesa Portales, she said, the one Dan took a few years ago.

Large-format camera, a black drop cloth over him, and whiskey in Dan's thermos. The weather was very pleasant on that day and I remember it fondly.

It will be wonderful, Veronica said, for your reputation. Everyone will want to know about your new project, everyone will want to see it.

You are inventing something out of nothing, I said. And I don't want anyone stepping foot on Mesa Portales. Your idea will only encourage them.

And in fact I was correct, as Fitz was inundated with interview and photo requests. After that Veronica put a lock on the gate and also told Fitz that I was not available for interviews because I was traveling abroad to Rio de Janeiro for inspiration. That's ridiculous, I said, as I would never visit Rio de Janeiro. It's far too humid there, and I've heard the mosquitos are terrible. You should have thought of somewhere else to send me, such as Quito or possibly Valparaíso.

Veronica arranged for Dan and his graduate students to oversee and execute what she called *Home: Unmaking* by Agatha Smithson. One of the graduate students would bring a camera to photograph my house and also its taking down. Proper documentation is important in this kind of work, Veronica said. Also you will have pictures to look at later and remember.

But I find no life or satisfaction in photographs, and I told Veronica so. Yet not long after that she brought me a snapshot that she found in a box at Alice's house. She presented it to me with smug pomp, as if to prove something.

This photograph is old, four inches square with a white border, and is riddled with small white flecks, as if no one had bothered to clean the negative before printing it. The craggy rock near the far end of the ocean canyon is visible in the background. In the foreground, on top of Mesa Portales, a man in work clothes talks to a young woman in a dress and dusty boots. Behind them other men are crouched over, working, and there is a scattering of trowels and brushes and collection boxes. The shadows are deep and black, and the woman has raised her hand to shield her eyes from the sun. Overall there is a sense of motion, a slight blurring of each figure. But in the far corner of the frame is a small child standing quietly with its back to the camera, the outline of its body sharp and clear, looking out over the ocean canyon.

They were collecting artifacts up here, Veronica said. Arrowheads, maybe pottery.

Stolen, I said. Dead in a drawer somewhere.

I slid the photograph into my back pocket and said no more about it. But I look at it often now, because despite what I said to Veronica about photographs, it's true that the small child in the corner of the frame is still alive to me.

♦ ♦ ♦

IT WAS AGREED THAT DAN and the graduate students would come to Mesa Portales in late fall.

You can stay with us at Alice's house while they're taking your house down, Veronica said. I can interview you for the biography, we'll have plenty of time to get started.

I will stay at Mesa Portales, I told her. I will sleep in the back of my pickup.

She didn't argue, as there would be no point to that. But what about afterward? she said. It'll be almost winter by then, Agatha.

In the weeks before Dan and the graduate students arrived, Veronica brought me new frames and canvases. Her cheeks pinked from the exertion of preparing them, and when she finished I sent her away immediately.

I pulped Alice's letters. I did this in my metal tub. First the water turned gray and, after that, a very pale and luminous yellow. I didn't have a wash for days, but it turned out perfectly, the pulp, a neutral in every way, yet also not neutral at all. Veronica primed more canvases, and I spread a very thin layer of pulp over each one, and let them dry in the sun. After that I proceeded as usual, with exact pencil lines and tiny, feathery brushstrokes that became repeating horizons of warm color. They were different, these paintings, because I thought of Alice while I did them. I had never done such a thing before.

These paintings are not masterpieces. I would laugh at anyone who said such a thing. In fact they are infected with a secret sentimentality that has meaning only for me. They are my greatest failure and greatest folly; but oh, how I love them. In this regard it seems I have become a sentimental person after all. I wonder what Georgia would think of that.

Still I make sure to scoff at Veronica, cruelly, when she suggests that these paintings are my best work yet. It makes me doubt her scholarship entirely. She takes my comments with grace, but I know that later she'll scribble in her notebook about me, about the paintings, maybe even about what has happened at Mesa Portales. She may well end up with a book about me, but she should be careful what she writes because, after all, I am the one with the shark-lawyer.

These canvases will not go to Fitz and are not to be sold. I've donated them to the permanent collection of the Wheeler Museum in Taos, and they will hang there in their own dedicated gallery room forever. It is all arranged and sealed in contracts written by the museum and the shark-lawyer and signed by me. Veronica carried all the paperwork to and fro and hand-delivered the paintings to the curator, who naturally felt that the museum had won a kind of lottery that it hadn't even known was going on.

I won't attend the Wheeler opening because I will be in Rio de Janeiro. Veronica says she'll bring more canvases and paint to Mesa Portales, and that I must keep working. She is excited about the factory she thinks we're operating here. In fact she has a gleam in her eye. I recognize that gleam: it is the gleam of the upper hand. But I have no intention of letting her have it forever.

VERONICA BROUGHT JOSEY, THAT LAST time he came to Mesa Portales. He got out of her car with the chicken-lawyer's clock, and I was overjoyed to see him. Veronica said she had taken charge of his education and arranged with his mother that he start at a boarding school in Santa Fe. He deserves a better education than he can get around here, she said.

I bit my tongue; it was a first. What do you think about boarding school, Josey?

He gathered up the cat in his arms and looked down at it. I don't know yet, he said.

The way he said this gave me pain. It will be an uprooting, and no one can say how it will go. It is hard to be a child in this world. If I have regrets about various things that I have done, they are for Josey.

Before he left he told me that Saturday evenings his mother now walks across their property on her way to the new beau's house, and she passes his father's grave as she comes and goes. On Sunday mornings Josey watches for her walking back up through the pasture. She enters the house with the fresh dawn air and says, Why aren't you ready for church? and they laugh together because they never go to church and never would.

Also Josey said his mother will be having a baby in the spring. It'll be nice, he said, a baby.

Yes, I said. A baby is nice.

DAN AND THE GRADUATE STUDENTS arrived in mid-November to take down my house.

First they dismantled the roof and removed the windowpanes and the door. After that they took pickaxes to the bricks. Every day there was less house, and Dan suggested that they scatter the broken bricks on the land around Mesa Portales, so that it will be rare to stumble across one, and also so that the bricks will eventually dissolve back into the earth.

In the evenings the graduate students did that, they loaded up the pickups and drove down the mesa and then off the road in different directions, stopping now and then to unload bricks before driving a little farther on and doing it again, until the flatbeds were empty. Then they would turn off the engines and let down the tailgates or perch on the cabs, drink beer and watch the sun go down.

Dan and I watched them from the top of Mesa Portales; we could see them from far away and their voices came to us in snippets, sometimes a laugh or word or two. When it was dark Dan lit the lantern on the southeast corner of the mesa, so they could orient themselves and find their way back to the road.

On the last day of this work we woke to the first snow. I stood on the ledge and admired the ocean canyon decked in white.

Dan unzipped his sleeping bag and joined me on the ledge. The sun was at our backs, our breath was misty before us. We watched the light rise higher and fill the ocean canyon. Underneath the sage and piñon was clay, layers of sandstone and shale, limestone, fossils, bones and seeds long petrified. Always there has been the end of one thing and the beginning of another. Also I felt the new line—a soft line, not impenetrable—that shimmered in the air between Dan and me. I appreciate the beauty of a line, there is no way not to, and I understood that I would have to let go of Dan a little, in order that we both move forward.

He asked, was it difficult to see the house gone?

But I have never regretted doing things that must be done, and I told him this.

Also I said to him, Congratulations.

He looked surprised. What for?

For your beautiful baby, I said, and patted his shoulder. For Margot.

Oh, he said, and smiled. Thank you, Agatha.

We watched as the graduate students began to emerge from their tents, how they yawned and looked around for breakfast.

What will you do now? Dan asked me. Where will you go?

I don't know yet, I said.

He nodded. Why don't you tell me when you decide, just in case. So I'll know.

Once the sun was up, we made a fire and ate our breakfast, and after that Dan and the graduate students packed their things and drove away with the windowpanes wrapped in blankets for salvage. I turned back toward the ocean canyon, the house once again perfect in my head.

AFTER THEY WERE GONE I threw my bedroll in the back of the pickup and laid Alice's cane across the seat. I sat on the ledge one more time. But my mind was in a jumble over leaving, and I felt Alice behind me. I did not know how to say good-bye to any of it.

And then I had my last visitor at Mesa Portales.

I heard a car coming and guessed that it would be Veronica. But it was not.

This visitor drove her pickup near me and got out. She stood very straight and strong, with lovely dark hair arranged in a low twist at the nape of her neck. She wore jeans and cowboy boots and a flannel jacket, and she was altogether pleasing. She was not a person I had ever seen before.

Who are you? I said.

She laughed, and the tender tone of it sent a thrill of recognition through me. It was a laugh that I have known before.

I'm Lorna, she said.

IT IS RARE IN LIFE that one receives such a shock. We must appreciate these shocks when they come to us, as they are invigorating and keep us alive in this world. I found that I was standing and that my mouth was hanging open. Well, I gathered up my jaw and sat back down on my stool.

Lorna stood at her mother's grave. We didn't either of us say a word. The flowers from the funeral had long ago blown away in the wind, but the postmistress's bouquet was sturdier and still in its place. Lorna wiped away a few tears and bent down to examine the dried apple-flowers. She whispered something to Alice. Then she walked to the ledge, shielded her eyes from the sun, and looked out over the ocean canyon.

I tried to think of how this Lorna could be possible. I looked at her carefully. She had freckles on her cheeks, a small scar on her forehead, a man's watch on one narrow wrist. Her fingernails were bitten to the quick. I searched for and saw the flutter of pulse at her throat.

I got up to stand closer.

She looked over at me. She tucked a loose strand of hair behind her ear, she coughed slightly and rubbed her nose. I watched her chest rise up and down with each breath, how she stood firmly on the ground. In fact she was solid and blocked the view.

They said you had a house up here, she said, but where is it? I sure don't see one.

I took it down, I said. Your mother didn't like it.

Lorna took a cigarette from her pocket and lit it. This was not an easy job on top of a mesa in the breeze, but she did it twice and offered one to me.

I accepted the cigarette, but also I caught her wrist with my other hand, in order to feel her skin and bone: to be sure of her.

She looked at my hand on her wrist. You didn't know?

I didn't know, I said.

I ASKED THE MOST IMPORTANT question first. I said, Did your mother know?

At that Lorna laughed, a bitter laugh. Of course she knew, she said.

I stood silent, suffering, because Alice had not told me about this Lorna. I stared across the ocean canyon at the prickly pear, which had faded in the cold to a dull olive brown. It would green up in spring, but I would not be around to see it.

Finally I said, So you're not in the coffin.

I'm not in the coffin, she said.

Then who is?

I could see that she didn't like this question. She pressed her lips together, as if making sure no words escaped. She looked away.

But I wouldn't let her off so easily. Josey and I had dug up this coffin, we had gone to no small trouble because we thought Lorna was in it, and the effort had cost us; perhaps it had cost Josey most of all.

So I asked again, Who is in your coffin?

I could feel that she was deliberating inside herself. Then the light over the ocean canyon shifted and so did Lorna. She looked straight at me, and once she began looking, she didn't waver. Whatever had happened to her as a girl, I could see that she was now a person who did not yield unless she cared to.

A different girl, she said. Not me.

I waited. For the first time I was the person who could not endure a silence. Why? I asked.

To get away from a man, she said. I thought he'd kill me one day. Well, one day I unlocked my front door and found he'd killed another girl first. I called Ma from the kitchen. I kept dropping the phone because my hands were shaking so bad. Finally I stayed down on the linoleum with the phone to my ear. Calm down, honey, calm down, honey. Ma was saying it to both of us. Then we just breathed with each other for a while. All the time I could feel the girl in the living room, just on the other side of the wall.

Lorna stopped and glanced at Alice's grave. Then Ma cleared her throat and coughed. She hacked, it was a terrible noise, like trying to get rid of something caught. After that her voice was like listening to a different person.

She looked at me as if wondering if I had heard that voice of Alice's, but I shook my head.

I did what Ma told me, Lorna said. She said he would get away with it and that I'd be next, that things always went that way. She said, Wait in the house until dark, and Curley will come get you. But I was too afraid to be inside with the girl, so I crawled under the front porch until I saw Curley's car pull up. Ma sent Pops off on a hunting trip, then called my neighbor and said, I haven't heard from my daughter in a couple days, and can you check on her? Ma identified the body and said it was me. No one believed the man when he said it wasn't. By then I was in Arizona.

It was impossible not to be startled by this news, but also I was filled with admiration and pride at Alice's secret daring, which I had never imagined.

Curley was working for the district attorney in Albuquerque at the time, Lorna said. The day will never come when he's stopped being proud of how he papered it all over.

Who is this Curley? I asked.

A friend from grade school, she said. He ended up back here, you must have met him. He likes to know everything about everyone and hoard it up for later.

Curley? I said. Ha!

He has never told a soul, she said. Neither has Ilona.

This information stopped me in my tracks: that both the chicken-lawyer and the postmistress had known Alice's secret while I had not.

Well, why give the whole show away to a stranger now? I said.

I heard you're not a stranger, she said.

This was one of the kindest things ever said to me by anyone, and

I smoked the rest of my cigarette in silence, because I wanted to let Lorna's words linger in the air.

Lorna dropped her cigarette butt onto the ground. I guess we'd all end up in jail if it got out.

Maybe not around here you wouldn't, I said.

They didn't want to take that chance, Lorna said. And no one wanted Pops to know. Later I asked Curley where the girl's body was, what had become of her, and was her family looking for her? He said that he never knew who she was and that he wasn't going to get caught trying to find out. Ma had the girl buried in the backyard before Pops got back from his hunting trip.

I thought of Alice's backyard, its unnatural qualities. I knew that Veronica would not bother with any gardening whatsoever, and that everything would slowly grow over and liberate itself.

Lorna said, Once everyone was used to me being dead, Ilona wrote to me care of the post office in Gallup: *Can I tell your mother a package will arrive on such and such a date?* She'd watch for my reply. I used to drive up here on the back road, and Ilona and Ma would walk up to meet me. But after a while I threw out Ilona's letters without reading them. I made sure to never have a phone line.

Her eyes glittered. Curley came to see me. He said the right and wrong of it was complicated but that Ma had wanted to give me a new chance. But it didn't feel like one. After a while I didn't want to see any of them from home anymore. That poor girl was dead and her family didn't even know it. I couldn't bear it for me and I couldn't bear it for her.

Your mother was trying to save you, I said.

Well, she didn't, Lorna said. I can't ever come home. I'm as good as a ghost. Ma understood that I was the same as her, but she didn't know how to fix it.

I bristled for Alice. That's a hard take, I said.

You're misunderstanding, Lorna said. I know what her life was like. I can feel more than one way about her.

I thought about all this. I did not say a word while I was thinking.

In the end I had one thought, which I did not care for: I did not know Alice after all.

I said this thought out loud.

That's your pride talking, Lorna said, giving me a disappointed look. You can't know everything about a person, and why should you?

I scowled, because who was this daughter, lecturing to me?

Ma forgot that I was alive, Lorna said. I suppose she saw the grave every day, and as time went on, she didn't doubt it. Ilona wanted me to visit; she tried to get me to come. But the truth is I lost the habit of family. Most days I don't regret it.

I nodded, because these were things I understood.

She looked me in the eye. Ilona says Ma loved you. Maybe I didn't know my mother that well either. So you see we are in the same boat.

We stayed quiet for a few minutes.

Where did you go to? I asked finally. Where have you been?

Not far. No one was looking for me anyway. Window Rock area.

With your Navajo boy?

She frowned at me. His name is Ivan Roanhorse, and he is not a boy. But no, not with him. Not then and not now.

I offered her a sandwich that Dan had left me with, but she shook her head.

She looked at me then, very seriously. Your house is gone, so I guess you're leaving. I don't like how Ma's all alone up here. She never liked to be alone. But I guess it's better than the Presbyterian cemetery next to Pops. Maybe I can be buried up here with her one day.

I bit my tongue so as not to say that until this very day, in fact until this very hour, I had thought that Lorna was already with her!

Before Lorna left Mesa Portales, I asked her, What about Frank Jr.?

She shook her head. He's accustomed to me being dead, she said. Maybe I shouldn't stir it up. I can't tell what might happen.

Briefly I looked over at Alice's grave and I thought about this, about being accustomed to the idea of people being dead. Then I looked back at Lorna.

I think you should go see him, I said. It might be good, what's stirred up. You might be glad of it.

I don't know, she said. Maybe.

WHEN LORNA LEFT MESA PORTALES, she said she would not be back. I collected our cigarette butts and buried them on the ledge. To the southwest the clouds were breaking up. Perhaps it would shine on Pie Town. I was empty and also full, and I did not know what to think of any of it.

I lay down on the ground to rest, as Lorna had taken all the punch out of me. I turned my head in the direction of Alice's grave. I stretched my arm out toward her. Had we been an honest pair? There was no one to ask or answer. I closed my eyes and thought with all my heart, and the answer that came back to me was *Yes*.

Then I got in my pickup and left Mesa Portales. I won't be back, because going back to Mesa Portales is not a thing that I can bear to do. In fact I plan to travel in my pickup wherever I like, all winter and spring. But I'll come in the summer to see Josey, when he is home from boarding school. I hope there will be things I can do for him, because I will do them all.

Also I'll make sure to call on the chicken-lawyer to inform him that I also know the secret, and therefore he has no standing to feel superior over me. I'll instruct him to transfer the Mesa Portales property to Lorna, in whatever name she now goes by. Perhaps one day, if she wants, she can be the stranger come to town.

Veronica will soon figure out where to look for me, as she is a very deducing person. I want Lorna to have the thunderbird brooch, and so in Alcie's room I wrap it in two layers of brown paper. On the inner layer I write, *For Lorna*, and on the outer layer, *For the Postmistress*. I give this package to Francesca, with instructions to give it to Veronica when she comes searching for me.

I didn't know that girl was a postmistress, Francesca says. Where should I tell her you went off to.

Tell her I went to Rio de Janeiro, I say, but also to keep an eye out for me when the lilacs bloom this year.

It's hard to believe a word that comes out of your mouth, Francesca says. But then she smiles at me, like a promise.

Lately I've thought more about Ma Binney and her widows, of how I am now a kind of widow. Georgia has been one for a long time already. I would like to see Georgia's deep wrinkles when she laughs and enjoy how she is serious in her talk and serious in her jokes, and how she turns frosty when she feels imposed upon. But Georgia and I may never see each other again, and in this way it is sad to grow old.

Or perhaps I will go see Georgia one day and offer amends as other people do, and then we may not be quite as sorry to be growing old together.

What is true in every moment? Nothing we can ever have again. I can't overcome my tender knees, my heart that shudders now and again, my breath that sometimes fails me in the evening. I walk out to the porch and stand next to the old man in his chair. We nod at each other and look at the snow-covered mountains spread out before us. The air is cold, the sun is hot. It is easy in moments of beauty to think of nothing other than what is in front of me. But all other moments are difficult ones.

At night I imagine myself in my house on Mesa Portales, looking out over the ocean canyon, like a soaring bird come to rest on a perch.

I have never truly grieved the death of anyone. What would be the point of that? It seems a horror to avoid if one can, and I always can. Yet lately I wonder if something has gone wrong in my habits. Perhaps there is some softening in my brain, in the way that I feel things. If this is growing old, I won't have it. In fact I reject it outright. But also I laugh at myself, because how can I reject growing old if I want to live?

Author's Note

THIS NOVEL WAS LOOSELY INSPIRED by a period in the life of the painter Agnes Martin (1912–2004), who, in 1967, quit painting and left New York City—and then eighteen months later turned up in northern New Mexico. She built an adobe house at Mesa Portales and lived a hermit's existence for nearly a decade; during that same time, I spent much of my childhood visiting my grandparents in the house where my mother grew up, not far from where Martin was living. Martin began painting again in the early 1970s, moved to Galisteo and then to Taos, and went on to international renown. An offhand, ambiguous remark my grandmother made years later— involving Martin, a packet of destroyed letters, and my grandmother's best friend—planted a seed and gave me something to think about on and off for years. Although aspects of Martin's life and art are points of departure for this novel, I've invented all the rest of it, and have also taken some liberties with the landscape of the Mesa Portales area.

My appreciation for Martin's work has come about by simply standing in front of it, at any opportunity, and looking. For me there has been no better place to do this than the Agnes Martin Gallery at the Harwood Museum of Art in Taos, New Mexico. There are also many beautiful and thoughtful books about Martin. A handful of my favorites are *Agnes Martin: Independence of Mind* edited by Chelsea Weathers (Radius Books), *Agnes Martin* edited by Frances Morris and Tiffany Bell (D.A.P./Tate), *Agnes Martin and Me* by Donald Woodman (Lyon Artbooks), and *Agnes Martin: Her Life and Art* by Nancy Princenthal (Thames & Hudson).

My thanks to Bonnie Steward at the Georgia O'Keeffe Museum Library & Archive in Santa Fe, New Mexico, who graciously organized books, materials, and clippings for me to look over, including copies of six handwritten letters Martin wrote to O'Keeffe in the early 1950s (the originals are at Yale University's Beinecke Rare Book & Manuscript Library). Martin's letters revealed hopes for an international freight boat trip with O'Keeffe—a trip that never happened—and I used this detail in Agatha's description of her friendship with O'Keeffe. All inventions and any errors related to O'Keeffe's actual life and history are mine alone.

Acknowledgments

THANK YOU TO MY AGENT, Susan Golomb, for encouragement, guidance, and straight talk. Also to my editor, Amy Guay, whose vision and thoughtful questions led the way; and to Eva Kerins and everyone at Avid Reader Press. Sasha Landauer and Peggy Boulos Smith at Writers House, thank you. Also many thanks to Rowan Cope, Mehar Anaokar, and everyone at Serpent's Tail.

Heartfelt thanks and love always to Kevin, Miles, and Stella Lee. Also to the late Robert Kabak, for the great pleasure of his paintings.

Thank you, Eileen Garvin, for your insights and friendship. To Magda Bogin and Under the Volcano; to Ayşegül Savaş, Jim Shepard, and Hannah Tinti; and to Hedgebrook for the time at Waterfall Cottage. Thank you, Robin McLean and Dona Bolding, for enthusiastic reads at the beginning and end.

To my parents, John and Mary-Ethel, and my sisters, Margaret and Lizzie. Liz Blazer, Jeff Oliver, Corrine Johnson, Peg Bogard, Elise Bradbury, and Angie Lee: Thank you. A special salute to the late Lexie Shabel; if you knew her, you understand.